MW01474761

Promise Date: 05-DEC-23 (TUE)   Promise Date: 05-DEC-23 (TUE)

765742LV00025B/31
CDS4:BLACKSTD
DIGIJACKETGRAY

765742LVX00115B - 765742LVX00118B [4 : 6]

765742LV00025B

BOOK
STBW19_SM   CONTAINS: MONC

GLOSS JACKET

Department	Operator's Name (Please print)
Printing	
Binding	
Cutting	
Shipping	
Batch Location	

765742LV

Promise Date: 05-DEC-23 (T

Batch 765742LV00025B

765742LVX00115B DIGIJACKETBLUE	9781635110005 5.50X8.50	DEATH RIDES THE SURF 214 <C> 0.5 GLOSS (1)
765742LVX00116B DIGIJACKETBLUE	9780937912638 6.00X9.00	The Hos-Blethan Affair 656 <Q> 1.375 GLOSS (1)
765742LVX00117B DIGIJACKETGRAY	9781948155281 6.00X9.00	Across the Rhine: The Things Our Fathers 360 <H> 0.8125 GLOSS (1)
765742LVX00118B DIGIJACKETGRAY	9798988403166 6.00X9.00	Diary of a Psychosis: How Public Health 430 <J> 0.9375 GLOSS (3)

Praise for Noreen Wald

THE KATE KENNEDY MYSTERIES

"Sparkles like the South Florida sunshine…Kate Kennedy is a warm and funny heroine."
— Nancy Martin, Author of the Blackbird Sisters Mysteries

"Miss Marple with a modern twist…[Wald] is a very funny lady!"
— Donna Andrews, Author of the Meg Langslow Mysteries

"A stylish and sophisticated Miss Marple, seeking justice in sunny South Florida instead of a rainy English Village, and meeting the most delightfully eccentric suspects in the process."
— Victoria Thompson, Author of the Gaslight Mysteries

"Kate Kennedy's wry wit, genuine kindness, and openness to adventure make her a sleuth to cherish. *Death is a Bargain* is another top-notch entry in a great series."
— Carolyn Hart, Author of the Death on Demand Mysteries

THE JAKE O'HARA MYSTERIES

"Murders multiply, but Jake proves up to the challenge. She sees through all the subterfuge and chicanery, solving a mind-boggling mystery in a burst of insight. All the characters are charmingly kooky and fun…a good beginning for a new series."
— *TheMysteryReader.com*

"[Wald] writes with a light touch."
— *New York Daily News*

"The author keeps the plot airy and the characters outlandish."
— *South Florida Sun-Sentinel*

DEATH RIDES THE SURF

Mysteries by Noreen Wald

The Kate Kennedy Series

DEATH WITH AN OCEAN VIEW (#1)
DEATH OF THE SWAMI SCHWARTZ (#2)
DEATH IS A BARGAIN (#3)
DEATH STORMS THE SHORE (#4)
DEATH RIDES THE SURF (#5)

The Jake O'Hara Series

GHOSTWRITER ANONYMOUS (#1)
THE LUCK OF THE GHOSTWRITER (#2)
A GHOSTWRITER TO DIE FOR (#3)
REMEMBRANCE OF GHOSTWRITERS PAST (#4)
GHOSTWRITER FOR HIRE (#5)

DEATH RIDES THE SURF

A KATE KENNEDY MYSTERY

Noreen Wald

DEATH RIDES THE SURF
A Kate Kennedy Mystery
Part of the Henery Press Mystery Collection

Second Edition
Hardcover edition | March 2016

Henery Press, LLC
www.henerypress.com

All rights reserved. No part of this book may be used or reproduced in any manner whatsoever, including internet usage, without written permission from Henery Press, LLC, except in the case of brief quotations embodied in critical articles and reviews.

Copyright © 2016 by Noreen Wald
Author photograph by Matthew Holler

This is a work of fiction. Any references to historical events, real people, or real locales are used fictitiously. Other names, characters, places, and incidents are the product of the author's imagination, and any resemblance to actual events or locales or persons, living or dead, is entirely coincidental.

ISBN-13: 978-1-63511-000-5

Printed in the United States of America

To Steve, with love

ACKNOWLEDGMENTS

My deepest thanks to Steve Smith. I literally couldn't have done this one without him. And thanks to the usual suspects: Donna Andrews, Carla Coupe, Ellen Crosby, Diane and Dave Dufour, Laura Durham, Barbara Giorgio, Peggy Hanson, Doris Holland, Susan Kavanagh, Valerie Patterson, Gail Prensky, Billy Reckdenwald, Pat Sanders, Dr. Diane Shirer, Gloria and Paul Stuart, Joyce Sweeney, and Sandi Wilson.

Thanks to the Henery Press team for putting new life into Jake and Kate. A special thanks to my lead editor, Rachel Jackson. The new covers designed by Kendel Lynn are great.

And a big thank you to my agent, Peter Rubie.

One

Monday evening, October 30

There were funerals where you knew, with cold certainty, that the corpse wouldn't be the only person you'd never see again. Kate Kennedy had just returned from one.

The deceased, Jane Kuloski Whitcomb, flew with Kate almost fifty years ago when they'd been stewardesses. Over the decades, they exchanged Christmas cards and photos of their kids, and met a few times when Jane would come back to New York to visit her mother.

Somehow Kate, who prided herself on her powers of observation, hadn't noticed Jane had become a practicing snob. Then last winter, Jane—who'd married a dermatologist, not a detective—moved from the Midwest to Palm Beach and attempted to revive their old friendship. Kate discovered that not only did they have nothing in common, she didn't even like Jane.

Of course, that awakening hadn't kept Kate from attending Jane's requiem mass, where she'd shared a pew with two of the other—and much more famous—Kennedy family cousins.

"Shriver or Smith?" Marlene Friedman, Kate's forever best friend and former sister-in-law, sounded like Chris Matthews as she and Kate strolled down Neptune Boulevard, trying to walk off calories after devouring platters of fried shrimp and hot fudge sundaes at dinner.

Kate picked up the pace. "I'm not sure. They all look alike to me. Lots of teeth. I think the young man—well, he must be in his forties—might have been one of Bobby's brood."

A pale gold harvest moon rose in the early evening sky. The moist, salty air held a hint of South Florida autumn, as waves on either side of them crashed against the beach.

Under the spotlights, one of the two guys at the end of the pier appeared to be struggling with a large fish. A bearded, younger man stowed bait and beer in a small motorboat. A mellow Frank Sinatra sang "My Way," but the lyrics faded out as Kate and Marlene approached the men. The bearded man waved. He looked familiar. Probably a regular at the Neptune Inn.

Kate waved back. Sometime over the last year, after the intense, constant grieving for Charlie—who'd never lived in the condo he'd chosen—had morphed into a dull ache, always with her but bearable, Palmetto Beach had become home.

Marlene shook her head, her platinum twist holding firm in the sea breeze. "Really, an honest-to-God celebrity sighting and you can't even identify which Kennedy you saw."

"I was at a funeral, Marlene." Kate laughed. "I couldn't ask for an autograph."

Marlene's frustrated expression indicated that was exactly what Kate should have done. "So, if you didn't relate to any of the mourners, maybe I would. Widower Whitcomb walks, talks, *and* has money, right? How bad can he be? And I could use a chemical peel. A dermatologist's almost as good as a plastic surgeon."

Kate laughed. She and Marlene had put Kate's granddaughter Katharine's unrequited love story on hold during dinner, though Marlene did report on her morning visit to the boy's grandmother who ran the only tanning salon/talking skull operation in South Florida.

"Shark!" The slimmer of the two fishermen standing at the edge of the pier dropped his pole. "Jesus Christ. Is that blood?"

The motor on the small boat revved up, and the bearded young man at the tiller veered south toward what appeared to be, by the light of the moon, a body floating face down.

"Call 911, quick!" the slim fisherman yelled, and then hopped into the bearded young man's moving boat.

The heavy set man peered into the water. "Looks like one of them goddamn surfers." He gestured toward the beach. "That's a piece of his board over there."

As the man punched in the numbers on his cell phone, Marlene screamed. An ungodly, piercing wail. Kate watched in horror as the bearded man stopped the boat and the slim man reached over port side into the sea and pulled a bloody stump on board.

Two

Two nights earlier, Saturday, October 28

"I hate school, I hate my mother, and I hate being a virgin," Katharine Kennedy said. "Please don't tell me to go home. I'm moving to Florida, Auntie Marlene, and I'm shedding excess baggage: classes, college, chastity. I know you of all people will understand and support me. And I need you to intercede with Nana. I'll live at Ocean Vista till I find a job. In the cab from the airport, I passed a help-wanted sign. Pink Platinum is hiring."

Starting over? As a lap dancer?

Katharine had just turned eighteen. If Marlene provided refuge for her best friend's granddaughter, Kate would kill her.

"Jennifer and Kevin must be worried sick, Katharine. Let's call them. Then you can stay here for fall break while we sort this out."

The girl's freckled face flushed, her auburn curls

bouncing as she shook her head. "If you turn me in to my parents, Auntie Marlene, I might be forced to tell Nana about you."

Good God! Could Katharine somehow have discovered that her now dead and revered grandfather, Charlie, and her "Auntie Marlene" once had a four-martini fling almost a half century ago?

Katharine smiled, then gestured toward the hallway. "Shall I put my bags in the guest room?"

Like a flamboyant, frightened Willie Loman, Marlene rehearsed what she would say, determined to sell her best friend on the idea of her granddaughter moving in.

With Marlene's checkered past, Katharine might have unearthed any number of unsavory secrets, but that brief boozy bedding of her best friend's husband atop a pile of coats during a cocktail party had always led Marlene's guilt parade. The act of adultery should top her long list of sins, considering she'd been engaged to Charlie's twin brother at the time. A doubleheader, commandment-breaking, grievous matter. A mortal sin, even if she wasn't Catholic. A sin she fully expected to go to hell for, unless God had a sense of humor and had sent Katharine here as a kind of hell-on-earth punishment.

If Marlene could find out why Katharine was really here, lying to Kate might be easier. Based on her own experience, she felt certain there must be a man in the picture. Marlene's heart ached at the thought of her beloved Katharine chasing after some guy, then being hurt if he rejected her.

Men, not money, were the root of all evil. Marlene laughed. Maybe she should have that embroidered on a pillowcase or a t-shirt; she'd probably sell a million of them.

Putting her past on hold—three marriages, six

engagements, and she'd need a calculator to add up the total number of men she'd dated—Marlene picked up the phone and presented her pitch to Kate.

"I still don't understand. Why did Katharine come here?" Kate asked.

With decades of experience, Marlene translated. Kate was really asking why Katharine had shown up at Marlene's condo door instead of at her grandmother's. So Marlene, though she seldom did, measured her response. "Oh Kate, your granddaughter knows I'm a sucker for a sob story. You might have sent her packing."

"And you think I should let her stay?"

"Well, yes. Katharine's not herself. Something is eating at her. Something serious. We need to find out what's wrong. That may take a few days."

"She hasn't been returning my phone calls." Kate sighed. "I figured she was caught up in college life. A school as large as NYU can be overwhelming and, you know, she's living on her own with a roommate in the West Village. I almost wish she'd followed Lauren's lead and gone to Harvard, but she so wanted to study theater." Marlene could hear the worry in Kate's voice. She took a sip of Scotch, wishing she had a cigarette. "Come on, Kate. Lauren's smart and beautiful, but she has no spark. She's like your stuffy in-laws, the Lowells. Katharine's not only the spitting image of her father and grandfather, she inherited their spirit as well. And like Charlie, your granddaughter's a real New Yorker. She'd have hated Harvard."

"It doesn't sound as if she's happy at NYU either."

"I don't think her problem has anything to do with geography, Kate."

"Then why did she run away to Florida? Why is she

talking about finding a job here? Why would a *real* New Yorker leave the city she loves?"

"*Cherchez l'homme.*" Marlene's accent sounded more Queens than Paris.

"A man?" Kate's voice rose. "She's barely eighteen. How can you think Katharine came to Florida because of a man?"

"Are you so old you don't remember your seventeenth summer, Kate? You spent a hell of a lot of time under the boardwalk at Rockaway, doing God knows what with that Latin lover from Ridgewood."

Dead silence. Had Marlene gone too far? She counted to ten. Nothing but silence. She plunged. "Come back, Kate. I feel like I'm talking to myself here."

"Okay." Kate sounded resigned. "Tell Katharine she can stay with me. You and I will figure out how to deal with Jennifer and Kevin. Then we'll figure out who this man is and why Katharine followed him to Florida."

Three

Ballou always knew when Kate needed comforting. She hung up after talking to Marlene and the little white Westie settled in at her feet, licking her left hand.

Though Kate hated to admit it, Marlene might be right about Katharine. The girl had been acting strangely ever since she started college. No wait, even before that. Ever since late July when Katharine had returned from a week in Acapulco. On the telephone, her bouncy voice had taken on an edge of sadness and the stories she'd once shared so openly with her grandmother seemed edited.

Maybe all teenagers abridged their adventures sooner or later. Still, Kate had sensed a secretiveness that might well have stemmed from a budding romance. Had Katharine met a man in Mexico? Kate thought about a young woman who'd vanished while vacationing in Acapulco over the summer. Her mother was still all over TV, pleading for information. God, that could have been Katharine.

Kate petted Ballou, running her fingers through his soft

fur, grateful for his devotion. His feelings were never shrouded in secrecy.

Kate sighed. Stop it. What had she expected? To be privy to her granddaughter's sex life? She felt herself flush, watching her pale arm redden, the fine hairs standing straight up. Odd how only the hair on her head had turned silver while all her other body hair remained chestnut.

Here she was, staring at seventy, and Marlene could still strike a nerve with a crack about Kate's seventeenth summer. God, would she never grow up? Would she be worrying about what had or hadn't happened a lifetime ago?

She wondered if Marlene ever regretted her past, then realized there weren't enough hours in a day for her former sister-in-law to properly reflect on her long-ago transgressions. Kate laughed out loud, startling Ballou.

"Come on, Ballou, we're having company. Katharine's going to stay with us." The Westie loved her granddaughter. Kate could picture his excitement when the girl arrived. "Let's go make up the guest room bed."

Her white-on-white condo, decorated by Edmund, a doctor who moonlighted as an interior designer and her son Peter's partner, was as neat as if an anal-retentive owned it. Kate sighed; maybe one did. Bottom line: there were worse faults than always being prepared for a house guest. She would have to make a quick trip to the supermarket in the morning. Katharine liked bacon and eggs for breakfast.

And she'd call her son and daughter-in-law in the morning too. From what Marlene had said, Katharine was in her guest room, either sound asleep or feigning it, and Kevin and Jennifer weren't yet aware that their daughter had left New York. No sense getting everyone upset at bedtime.

A half hour later, Kate sat in an ecru terry cloth chaise on the balcony, sipping decaffeinated Lipton tea, Ballou at her side. A diamond tiara of stars sparkled atop a gold harvest moon in an inky sky, like priceless jewels displayed against a black velvet drape.

Chilled, she zipped up her blue cotton sweater, then reached for the teacup. How often had she shivered in South Florida? She could only recall one other time, that first lonely New Year's Eve after Charlie had died, when the sounds of revelers drifting up from the rec room and the bright moon and twinkling stars had left her cold and depressed.

Why had Katharine gone to Marlene? Kate felt hurt and, yes, damn it, jealous. The phone rang. Jumping up, she tripped over an indigent Ballou, dropping her favorite teacup, spilling its contents, covering her bare foot with tepid tea. But the Belleek cup didn't break. "Thank God for small favors," Kate said, her voice so cranky, Ballou stopped yelping.

"Hello," she grumbled into the phone, standing on one foot while trying to dry the other with a paper napkin, contorting her body into what felt like an advanced yoga position.

"And a pleasant good evening to you too, Kate." Nick Carbone, the oldest homicide detective in the Palmetto Beach Police Department, maybe the oldest in America, mocked her tone.

"It's after ten, Nick. Evening has turned into night." Gracious, wasn't she?

"And at your age, I guess you need your beauty sleep."

Ouch. Though overweight and often overbearing, Carbone was about a decade younger than Kate; tonight that statistic bothered her more than usual.

"Though I think you look great." He seemed sincere. Could that be possible? "Er, can you have lunch with me tomorrow? I thought we'd try Sea Watch. You like it there, right?"

How did Nick know that? She couldn't recall ever having mentioned it. And how could she say yes? Go out to lunch on Katharine's first day with her? If Kate accepted, it would be their third date, if what they were doing could be called dating. What the hell were they doing? A short, slim widow with enough mileage to accurately be described as a little old lady, still missing her dead husband, and a fat know-it-all detective with two ex-wives, fighting against retirement like Don Quixote tilting at windmills.

"Kate?" Nick's voice, Brooklyn brusque at best, sounded strained to the breaking point.

A surge of mixed messages flashed through Kate's mind, then tumbled off her tongue. "My granddaughter Katharine's here. At Marlene's, but she'll be with me tomorrow. I hate to leave her, but I would like to have lunch with you." Would she? She supposed so.

"Bring Katharine along, if she doesn't have other plans." Nick's voice had softened and was far less tense. "She's the redhead, right?"

"Yes, she looks just like her grandfather." Great, Kate, remind your *suitor* that you're still in love with your dead husband. Well, why not? She was, wasn't she?

"Okay. Let's see how it shakes out." The edge had returned. "Give me a call tomorrow morning. The early snowbirds have arrived. We'll need a reservation if we're going to Sea Watch." Nick hesitated, then added, "And why don't you invite Marlene too?"

A generous offer. Four for lunch at Sea Watch didn't

come cheap. And dragging her granddaughter and sister-in-law along made it definitely not a date.

"Thanks, Nick. That's very kind." She smiled as she heard the warmth in her own voice. "I'll call you either way."

She felt even better when Nick's good-bye returned the warmth.

The breeze coming from the open balcony door fluttered the sheer curtains. Kate put down the phone and stepped outside, straightening the cushion on the chaise and gathering up the teacup and saucer.

"Don't be stupid, man." A voice from the beach, loud and clear in the still of the night. A voice with a Cuban accent.

Kate crossed to the stone railing and stared out across Ocean Vista's swimming pool to the Atlantic. Rough tonight. She could hear waves crashing against the shore. The full moon served as a giant flashlight. Its glow, together with the lamps around the pool, softly illuminated the beach. She could make out two surfers and their surfboards at the water's edge.

The handsome Cuban and the surly, good-looking blond belonged to a group who called themselves the Four Boardsmen of the Apocalypse. They'd appeared about a month ago, chasing waves and driving Ocean Vista's owners crazy; however, since the beach belonged to the town of Palmetto Beach, the young men had as much right to ride the surf as the seniors had to swim or, in most cases, wade.

It must be close to midnight. Why would they be surfing at this hour?

A redhead ran along the shore, joined the boys, and wrapped her arms around the blond. Kate started. The moon shone on her granddaughter's face as Katharine locked lips with the surly surfer.

Four

One day earlier, Sunday, October 29

"I'm telling you, Marlene, Katharine was out on the beach at midnight." Kate pressed her Lipton tea bag against the china cup with such force it broke, scattering tiny leaves that floated on top of her tea like unwanted sprinkles on an ice cream cone. "I watched her from my balcony, cuddling up to that blond surfer, you know, the cute one, not the part-time lifeguard. Why does he surf in the middle of the night?"

She stood, crossed to the sink, dumped the tea, rinsed the cup, and started the brewing process from scratch. She'd just returned from church and felt guilty about her anger and resentment, though not enough for an attitude adjustment.

"Maybe the waves are better." Marlene stirred her coffee, her voice several decibels lower than usual. Katharine was still sleeping.

The sun streamed through the window in Marlene's kitchen, brightening the room but not Kate's mood.

After the second of last summer's two back-to-back hurricanes, Marlene's flooded condo had been completely renovated. But it hadn't taken Marlene, who'd dramatically downsized prior to the hurricanes, selling off her "treasures" from the fifties at the Palmetto Beach Flea Market, long to fill her new red, white, and blue kitchen with "more contemporary treasures." Kate had decided the eclectic look, while way too colorful for her taste, was not unattractive.

"Didn't you hear her go out?" Kate added a splash of milk, then sat down again at the washed pine table and reached for a bagel. She sounded critical, but she didn't care.

"I was watching *Leave Her to Heaven*. God, that Gene Tierney was a bitch."

"Focus, Marlene." Kate spread strawberry jam on one half of her bagel. She had no appetite, but these were freshly baked Einstein bagels, her favorite. Mary Frances Costello, a former nun and current Broward County tango champion, had dropped them off on her way up to her condo after the seven thirty mass.

"I am focusing." She sounded defensive. "I didn't hear her. So sue me."

Marlene wore a scarlet kimono that flattered her large frame, but her face, minus makeup, looked drawn, her platinum twist, usually unflappable, floundered, and several stray strands flopped about. Marlene frowned, pushing a bobby pin back into place.

"Katharine kissed him. If your theory is correct, that surly surfer must be the man she came here to find." Kate took a small bite, thinking an Einstein's bagel was almost as good as a New York bagel.

"She kissed him, huh?" Marlene smirked.

"You needn't look so pleased."

"Listen, Kate, your granddaughter's eighteen. Do you think he's the first guy she ever kissed?"

That was exactly what Kate thought, but she decided not to defend Katharine right now. She had too many questions and she needed Marlene's help. "If Katharine did come here because of that surfer, how do they know each other? Where could they have met?"

"Isn't that Fort Lauderdale's claim to fame? *Where the Boys Are.*" Marlene sang, smiling. A smug smile, Kate thought. "Katharine could have met him right here."

Kate shook her head. "She just arrived last night."

"Well, that's what she said." Marlene took another sip of coffee. "But maybe she's been down here a few days. Maybe she met surfer boy on the strip."

"Impossible. Jennifer calls Katharine every day. She'd know if her daughter had left New York."

"Would she?" Marlene taunted, seeming to enjoy playing devil's advocate. Did Marlene realize how much she was annoying Kate? Sometimes they acted as if they were still six years old, trying to out-hopscotch each other. "Katharine has a cell phone. She could have been answering from God-only-knows where when her mother called." Score one for Marlene.

"Or try this." Marlene, seemingly full of possibilities, rolled right on. "It's fall break. Maybe Jennifer and Kevin think Katharine's off visiting a friend."

Stumped and bothered by Marlene's scenarios, Kate said, "Katharine doesn't lie." Even before Marlene arched her right eyebrow, Kate realized her granddaughter's lie of omission would now force Kate and Marlene to lie to Jennifer and Kevin.

Marlene laughed. "She's lying like crazy, Kate. And we

need to find out the truth. Those surfers are sleazy. We can't have her befriending or bedding any of them. Though I have to admit the Cuban's mighty cute."

"How did Katharine get out of the condo and back in after her rendezvous on the beach last night?" Kate turned on the burner under the teakettle. She needed—no, she *craved*—the caffeine. "Miss Mitford locks up tighter than Fort Knox. Does our sentinel ever sleep?"

"She goes home at nine, sometimes ten, and is back at eight the next morning. I keep telling the board we're going to get in trouble over those long hours." Marlene had served as president of Ocean Vista's board of directors. Like most Broward County condo presidents, she'd taken her job very seriously.

"So Mitford couldn't have seen her or buzzed her back in."

"My key ring was on the table in the foyer." Marlene looked at the clutter and laughed. "Though how Katharine could have spotted it under all the mess remains a mystery. The girl must have her grandmother's genes."

Kate laughed too. It felt good. "Well, her grandfather was a homicide detective."

"No. I think she's a natural-born snoop like you."

"Is the key ring there now?"

"Yes, but with all the unopened bills, junk mail, straw hats, sunscreen bottles, and six copies of *People,* I can't tell if it's where I put it." Marlene eyed the junk piled on her kitchen table and shrugged.

"Right." Kate nodded, but didn't react. She'd gotten past her sister-in-law's constant state of clutter four or five decades ago.

"Should we just be direct with Katharine? Tell her you

saw her kissing Blondie on the beach? Maybe we could startle the truth out of her."

"Have you two been spying on me?" Katharine stood in the doorway, a scowl on her flushed freckled face and venom coating her question.

Five

After Katharine had locked herself in Marlene's guest bathroom, running the hot water until it steamed out from under the door, Kate called Mary Frances, the Liz Smith of Ocean Vista, to get the scoop on the surfers.

Three of the Four Boardsmen of the Apocalypse didn't have day jobs. Jon Michael, Katharine's crush, worked three nights a week as a bartender in a "gentleman's club." Good God, maybe at the Pink Platinum where Katharine hoped to get a job. Two of the boardsmen were Palmetto Beach born and bred. Jon Michael Tyler, the son of a single mother, lived with his grandmother, who ran a tanning salon, and Claude Jensen, another bronzed blond and a self-proclaimed cracker whose father was in jail. Claude had attended high school with Jon Michael. Though unemployed, Claude sometimes substituted for the lifeguard whose chair was only twenty-odd feet away from the gate leading to Ocean Vista's pool.

The third boardsman, Roberto Romero, a Cuban exile, was, in Mary Frances's words, as handsome as Fernando

Lamas had been when he swam with Esther Williams. How Roberto had landed in Palmetto Beach was a mystery. Where he got his money—he dressed in designer duds and surfed on a custom-made board—was a bigger mystery.

The fourth, Sam Meyers, the least skilled of the surfers, a tall, geeky guy from New Jersey, worked nights as a computer programmer and kept his fellow boardsmen supplied with beer and hot dogs from the Neptune Boulevard Pier.

"They all live to ride the waves. And they're all between eighteen and twenty-two." Mary Frances finished, breathless. For the dancing ex-nun, men were never too young or too old.

Kate thanked Mary Frances, searching for the off button on her new cell phone.

"What's your interest in those boys, Kate? Thinking about signing up for surfing lessons?" She giggled.

"You know, that's a great idea." Kate snapped the phone shut, rendering Mary Frances speechless.

She marched down the hall to the bathroom and banged on the bathroom door. "If you don't come out of there, young lady, I'm calling your mother and father. You're wasting time and money. If you continue to behave like a child, I'll treat you like one."

Marlene, on Kate's heels, shouted, "Don't force her."

Except for Marlene's dramatic outburst and the water still running full blast, Kate's threat was greeted by silence.

"Okay, Katharine. I have my phone ready and I have your mother on speed dial. I'm counting to five. That's Jennifer." Kate wasn't bluffing; she'd place the call. "One. Two. Three. Four."

The door opened. The steam heat almost bowled Kate over.

Her granddaughter, red as a lobster and wrapped in a purple towel, glared at Kate.

"Aunt Marlene said I can stay." A defiant Katharine swung her head toward Marlene, who started.

What was wrong with Marlene? Puzzled, Kate decided she couldn't be distracted. "Don't use that tone of voice with me, Katharine."

"Nana, I can't talk to Mom and Dad." Katharine sounded contrite, and something else. Frightened? Determined? "They'd never understand."

Sure she was being played, but wanting to find out what the devil was going on, Kate said, "Let's have a cup of tea, Katharine. I'm sure we can work this out."

The muscles in her granddaughter's jaw relaxed.

Marlene made pancakes and Katharine, who'd lost weight, too much in her grandmother's opinion, dug in like a stevedore. Kate took that as a sign that Katharine still believed her grandmother could somehow make everything okay.

On her fourth cup of tea of the morning, Kate decided to call her daughter-in-law and sell Jennifer on the idea of Katharine spending her fall break in Palmetto Beach. A week ought to buy them enough time to sort it all out.

Jennifer and Kevin weren't aware that Katharine had left New York City, but her daughter-in-law agreed to Kate's suggestion.

If Kate's plan worked out, maybe Katharine's parents would never have to know she'd run away from home. Not to mention classes, college, and chastity.

"Okay, I'll move to your condo this morning, Nana," Katharine said. "Just know I'm never going home. I'm getting a job and an apartment and I'm staying in Florida forever."

Right. Kate had six days to find out what the hell was going on and to get her granddaughter back to college.

"Darling, would you and Auntie Marlene like to have lunch with Nick and me?"

Katharine grinned, her grandfather Charlie's grin.

God, Kate hoped her invitation hadn't made it sound as if she and Nick Carbone were a couple.

Six

The Sea Watch Restaurant perched above the dunes on a wide expanse of sandy beach, a mile south of Ocean Vista. From their window table, the teal blue Atlantic seemed to stretch from here to eternity and soft, puffy clouds hovered over the whitecaps. Kate knew the food was as wonderful as the view. Snowbirds weren't yet in full flight, but at noon, the restaurant had no empty tables. Those without reservations waited at the bar.

Their waiter, a buff blond, asked, "What can I bring you guys?"

Kate cringed. When had that annoying way of waiters addressing customers reached South Florida?

Nick replied, "The three *ladies* will have piña coladas. And this *guy* will have a Scotch and soda."

Katharine smiled at Nick. Katharine damn well knew her parents would have ordered her a Diet Coke. Kate was surprised Carbone, a by-the-book detective, could break the law so cavalierly. But his gesture broke the ice as well. If Kate didn't like Katharine dating a surfer, her granddaughter hated the possibility of her grandmother being interested in any man other than Grandpa Charlie. Nick's treating Katharine like a grown-up had been a smart move. Not that Kate was all that interested in Nick.

And why did Marlene look so smug? Kate felt her cheeks redden.

The drinks arrived and they sipped in silence. Kate had prepped Marlene, providing her with an opening line that would distract and intrigue Katharine, who shared her grandmother's avid interest in crime and punishment. However, Marlene now nodding at a dapper seventy-something gentleman at the next table had missed her cue. Kate kicked her sister-in-law's foot, none too gently. "You wanted to ask Nick about..."

"Diamond Lil." Marlene pulled her meticulously lined and shadowed eyes away from Mr. Almost Right—at least number five hundred in that category—and batted them at Nick. "Any leads on that jewel-bedecked old broad who robbed the SunTrust Bank on Federal Highway and Kate's and my branch on Neptune Boulevard last week?"

Kate chimed in. "Mary Frances was depositing the Sunday collection from St. Paul's when Diamond Lil—catchy name the *Sun-Sentinel* dubbed the thief, isn't it?—pulled a gun in our bank and the teller, Mr. Porter, filled her knitting bag. Then the old lady grabbed Mary Frances's duffel. Over two thousand in cash, plus the parishioners' checks, which are probably useless."

Nick chuckled. "No. Not useless. Diamond Lil changed St. Paul's to Sutton Place Antiques and cashed one in Fort Lauderdale. Waved a driver's license at the antique dealer. The guy said he never suspected a nice old broad would be carrying a fake ID. So Lil got to buy herself yet another bracelet for two hundred dollars."

Nick almost sounded as if he admired the bank robber. Katharine giggled. "Does Diamond Lil wear lots of bling?"

The giggle warmed Kate's heart. "Yes. From her dangling earrings to her ankle bracelet. Both her sunglasses and her tiara are trimmed with rhinestones. But she dresses like a bag lady: a shapeless cardigan, in all this heat, and a wrinkled housedress as ancient as I am."

"Don't forget the torn sneakers." Marlene motioned to a copper-colored, dark-haired waiter. "I love the fashion statement of a rhinestone ankle bracelet worn over sweat socks."

Their new waiter smiled. "Another round, guys?"

"Hell no." Marlene handed him her empty glass. "This gal wants a double martini on the rocks."

The young man blushed. "Right away, ma'am."

"How many banks has this Diamond Lil hit?" Katharine asked.

"Three in Palm Beach County, plus the two here in Palmetto Beach," Nick growled, then yelled after the waiter. "Make that two double martinis."

Kate intercepted Katharine. "Don't even think about it. You're having a Diet Coke."

Mary Frances appeared at the table as dessert was being served. "Hi. I'm so glad to see you ladies. I had the most exhilarating morning." Her red hair grazed her shoulders, her emerald green eyes danced in the sunlight and her olive linen jumpsuit, deceptive in its simplicity, showed off her curves.

Marlene groaned and coughed to cover the sound. Katharine grinned and asked, "Where were you, Miss Costello?"

Nick stood and invited Mary Frances to join them. "Well just for a few minutes; I'm meeting my astrologist for lunch and a verbal tour of Venus."

"Can I come along for the ride?" Marlene asked.

Nick laughed, then asked the waiter to bring a chair over from a nearby table with only three diners. Ignoring Marlene, Mary Frances sat in Nick's empty chair.

Kate, admittedly a little jealous, admired their unexpected guest's creamy complexion. Could lifelong virginity be the solution for wrinkles?

Mary Frances Costello, who'd won the Broward County Tango Championship for two years in a row, looked more like Maureen O'Hara in *The Quiet Man* than like a sixty-year-old ex-nun.

According to Joe Sajak, widower and womanizer, during the weekly poker games in Ocean Vista's rec room, side bets were being placed on Mary Frances's virginity. The odds were two-to-one against. But Kate figured putting money on Mary Frances's chastity would be a safe bet. Maybe safer than betting on Katharine's.

"So where were you this morning, Miss Costello?" Katharine tried again.

Mary Frances beamed. "I had a private session with the world-famous talking skull." She paused for dramatic effect.

Kate watched as Nick's fleshy jaw dropped.

"His owner is based in Fort Lauderdale. She travels the world with Mandrake, you know, but they're in residence here for the summer. They just returned from a conference in Cairo. I was lucky to get an appointment. My astrologist's a personal friend of the skull and his owner."

Katharine stared at Mary Frances—Kate thought with amazement, but it could have been fear.

"For God sake's, Mary Frances!" Marlene banged on the table. "How can a former high school principal be such a superstitious sucker?"

Nick drained his glass, shaking his head—Kate guessed in disgust, not amazement.

"Miss Costello," Katharine's voice was shaky. "You spent the morning with Florita Flannigan?"

"Yes, I did, indeed." Mary Frances seemed pleased that Katharine had heard of the skull reader. "In addition to running Golden Glow, Palmetto Beach's best tanning salon, Florita reads skulls. For only fifty-five dollars, selected clients can enjoy private sessions with her crystal skull—reputed to have been found in an Aztec ruin—and get advice from the world beyond." Mary Frances ran her right hand through her hair, messing her curls just enough to make them flatter her more than ever.

Nick waved the waiter over. "Another martini here." He turned back to Mary Frances. "I know the place. The advertisements brag that Golden Glow is the only tanning salon/skull reading operation in Broward County. We're monitoring Mrs. Flannigan's activities very closely."

"Why?" Katharine asked. "Florita Flannigan is an honorable, hard-working woman."

"Have you met her?" Nick asked.

"Well, I haven't actually met her yet, but Mrs. Flannigan is my boyfriend Jon Michael's grandmother. He absolutely adores her."

Seven

Halloween was only two days away. Back in Rockville Centre, Long Island—where Kate and Charlie had lived for over forty years—the frost would be on the pumpkins and the neighborhood children would be stuffing scarecrows and getting costumes ready for trick-or-treating.

Ocean Vista's residents, some of them in their second childhoods, Kate thought uncharitably, were getting ready for Halloween. At last year's bash, the condo president had been found murdered on the beach. Kate didn't see how her neighbors could top that, but God knows they were trying, eagerly planning this evening's pre-Halloween picnic.

Instead of autumn leaves and sweater weather, the temperature at three o'clock hovered at eighty degrees. When Kate and Marlene returned from walking Ballou, the beach was awash with gossip about who would be going to the beach party as Sonny and Cher and how Joe Sajak had rented a Batman costume with extra padding in the tights.

The warm sea was capped with rough-for-South-Florida

waves and the surfers were driving some of the seniors out of the water.

Great, Kate thought as she sank into her beach chair, Ballou at her feet.

Three of the Four Boardsmen were in the surf. Kate watched Katharine try out a brand new surfboard, purchased on their way home from lunch. A wave knocked her granddaughter off the board and into the sea. Katharine screamed so loud Ballou, more than fifty feet away, barked. As Jon Michael helped Katharine back onto the board, Kate felt a pang of fear. Why? How could she feel such intense, collective dislike for young men she'd never met?

While shopping for the surfboard, Kate had asked about Jon Michael, feeling that was fair game since Katharine had blurted out at Sea Watch that he was her boyfriend. Other than admitting she'd met him in Acapulco and followed him here—"How convenient that they came to Palmetto Beach, Nana"—her granddaughter had supplied precious little information.

Kate gathered that Katharine had surprised her "boyfriend" last night. And maybe Jon Michael had been less than delighted to see her. She worried Katharine would be spurned. Or worse.

Marlene's questions had determined Katharine also met Claude, the local Palmetto Beach surfer, and Roberto, the Cuban, in Acapulco. Had the other young men been glad to see Katharine? Though Kate had missed them greeting each other, she doubted that.

More important: had the three surfers still been in Acapulco when that other young woman disappeared?

Ballou nuzzled Kate's left foot, comforting her. The Westie always sensed when she felt unsettled. She rubbed under Ballou's left ear and he licked her free hand. Kate squeezed her eyes shut, trying to stem the tears. Oh God, Charlie, I wish you were here. You'd know what to say to Katharine.

Marlene grabbed Kate's arm, shaking her. "Quick! Look out there in the ocean."

Kate's eyes flew open in time to see Jon Michael shove, and then hold, Katharine's head under the water as she flailed her arms about, splashing. The other blond surfer's loud cackle caused Kate to leap up and scream.

By the time Kate, Marlene, and Ballou reached the water's edge, Katharine had surfaced. She laughed off her grandmother's concern. "Oh Nana, I'm fine." Still, Katharine's voice seemed strained; perhaps her laughter was covering up anger. Directed at Kate? Or at Jon Michael, who stood, caressing his board like a lover, his gaze fixed on his feet? He needed a pedicure.

Since none of the young men made an attempt at introductions, she spoke up. "I'm Kate Kennedy, Katharine's grandmother, and this is our friend, Marlene Friedman." The Westie sniffed Jon Michael's left foot and moved on to smell his board. "And that's Ballou." Kate smiled as the little dog kicked sand on the surfboard.

A hand reached out. "My name is Roberto Romero. It is always a pleasure to meet two lovely señoras like you." Smooth as silk. Tall, dark, and handsome, with a Latin lilt and a sexy smile. Mary Frances was right. Roberto did evoke memories of Fernando Lamas in an old MGM musical.

He held Kate's eye for a moment, made an almost imperceptible bow, and then glanced toward the other surfers. "Jon Michael, where are your manners?" Roberto turned his attention back to Kate. "Señora Kennedy, please excuse Jon Michael, he is embarrassed—how you say?—his joke went too far."

"Yeah," Jon Michael mumbled. "Hey." His tanned, square face looked pained. No warmth in those ice blue eyes. He had great shoulders and biceps, must work out regularly. Kate offered her hand. His palm felt sweaty. The boy gave a weak shake, then dropped her hand, hoisted his board to his right shoulder, and stepped behind Katharine.

Yeah and *hey,* Kate thought. Jon Michael was quite the conversationalist.

The third surfer smiled, revealing yellow teeth, his left incisor missing. "I'm Claude, ma'am." The short, skinny boy appeared to be about sixteen, but Mary Frances had said that all the boardsmen were between eighteen and twenty-two. What idiot on the Palmetto Beach City Council had hired this kid as a substitute lifeguard?

Kate felt a fleeting moment of pity. The boy's blond hair had started to thin. His washed-out gray eyes were dull, almost blank. Had Claude Jensen shut down before leaving his teens? His red nose was peeling, almost raw, and his pasty skin would always burn, never tan. He spoke with a drawl. From Alabama, Kate guessed. Or maybe Florida's Redneck Riviera, abutting Alabama.

Claude's nod included Marlene. "Nice to meet y'all." He reached down and ruffled Ballou's fur. The Westie, who loved almost everyone, pulled away.

Marlene, who'd been unusually quiet, sighed. "Three Boardsmen down, one to meet."

Katharine scrunched her nose. "You promised me a surfing lesson, Jon Michael. Let's go." She waved dismissively, saying, "See you later, Nana and Auntie Marlene," over her shoulder. Her round bottom wiggled as she walked into the ocean. Jon Michael turned and, without a word, followed Katharine to the sea.

"Not to worry, Señora Kennedy," Roberto said. "Jon Michael is a strong swimmer and a great teacher. One day soon you will watch with pride as Katharine rides the waves."

Kate doubted that, but the Cuban seemed so sure and so sincere she smiled. "I hope you're right, Roberto."

"Just how did you land in South Florida, Roberto?"

Marlene came across like a brusque New Yorker. Well, of course, she *was* a brusque New Yorker, but tempered by a kind heart and generous soul. Right now neither her heart nor her soul was on the beach. Just her nose...which had smelled trouble.

Claude cackled, appearing ready to enjoy his fellow surfer's discomfort.

Roberto's charm never wavered. He grinned at Marlene, then spoke in his soft Latin lilt. "My mother and I fled from Cuba years ago. Our small boat was overcrowded. We were several miles from Deerfield Beach when the boat capsized."

Smooth, Kate thought. Too damn smooth.

"I dove for hours, trying to find my mother. To find anyone. But at thirteen I found myself alone in the Atlantic Ocean. I swam the rest of the way to shore and I kissed the sand. My *tia* Rosita in Miami took me in."

"Come on, we surfing or what?" Claude shoved the back of Roberto's head.

"If you ladies will excuse me, I must join my friends." Roberto nodded, picked up his surfboard, and followed Claude.

"Did you believe a word of that sob story?" Marlene shook her head.

"I'm going to ask Nick to check out Romero. Find out if

there's really an aunt in Miami." Kate had almost fallen for Roberto's glib patter.

Only the missing boardsman, Sam Meyers, had a real job. How did these young men fund their passion? Surfing in Acapulco costs money. Flying from Mexico to Florida didn't come cheap.

Jon Michael worked part-time as a bartender. If Claude had money, why didn't he have his teeth fixed? The well-groomed Roberto, who, according to Mary Frances, dressed in Armani, seemed to be the money man. Where did he get it?

Kate turned to Marlene. "Do you think Roberto's aunt is rich?"

"Aunt, my tush. I'll bet he's a kept man. Some old women will do anything for sex."

"Is that right, Marlene?" Kate laughed. It felt good.

Eight

The city of Palmetto Beach has a downtown that the natives referred to as the village center. One of the smallest downtowns in the USA, it stretches for one short and two long blocks from the Atlantic Ocean to the Neptune Boulevard Bridge which led to the mainland. West of the short block, abutting the beach and bisecting the village, A1A ran north and south.

Kate and Marlene, holding Ballou's leash, had showered and changed, and were on their way to the island's tiny supermarket. The store was located in a mini mall on the north side of Neptune Boulevard in the shadow of the bridge. Before grocery shopping, the two old friends planned to have ice cream sodas at Dinah's Restaurant next door to the supermarket, where Ballou and other small pets were welcome.

They'd crossed A1A and were waiting for the bridge traffic to abate before crossing the boulevard. A riot of red and pink hibiscus filled a small garden in front of the beauty salon. Unlike many of her Ocean Vista neighbors, Kate didn't think of Palmetto Beach as paradise, but it would suffice until she arrived there.

"I've been wondering about Acapulco." Kate adjusted her sunglasses. They seemed to spend more time on top of her silver hair than covering her eyes, but the sun was wickedly bright today.

"And my guess would be that you aren't considering a vacation there."

"What do you remember reading about that girl who disappeared there last summer? Amanda. I forget her last name."

"Rowling. A beautiful girl. Drama major at UCLA, you know. Her mother was on the *Today* show again just the other day." Marlene nudged Kate. "Come on, let's cross while we have the light."

The smell of the sea mixed with the fragrance of the flowers and the aroma of freshly baked bread that wafted from Dinah's. Heaven's scent couldn't be any better than this.

Suddenly starving, Kate opened the restaurant's front door and grabbed a window booth. She might have a blueberry muffin with her ice cream soda.

Strange how the mind and body could focus on mundane pleasures while the heart and soul fretted over major problems. Katharine's infatuation with Jon Michael might become a major problem. The loss of Charlie made Kate's heart ache every day, though the pain no longer throbbed. Nevertheless, she craved that muffin.

Most of the waitresses at Dinah's were Kate's and Marlene's age. A few needed the money, but several of them worked there because they loved their customers.

"Hi, girls. What'll you have?" Myrtle, blonde, brassy, seventy-six, and kicking—she was in a tap dance group the performed in assisted-living residences with Mary Frances—was all smiles. The crinkles around her eyes deepened. Their favorite waitress had the leathery skin of a woman who'd grown up in a beach town with year-round sunshine decades before there were any warnings about skin damage.

"A black-and-white ice cream soda and a blueberry muffin, please," Kate said, thinking she came across as defiant.

Marlene laughed. "Same for me."

Kate remembered them as eight-year-olds sitting at the counter of their candy store in Jackson Heights, sipping sodas, her mind and her heart grateful for their friendship. "When did Amanda Rowling disappear? I know it was after Katharine returned from Mexico."

"Late August." Marlene petted Ballou who sat at her feet, behaving like the gentleman he was. "Between our two back-to-back hurricanes. That's why we missed most of the original TV coverage; we were a tad busy picking up the pieces."

"I wonder when the three boardsmen returned from Acapulco."

"Well, they didn't show up on our beach until after Labor Day, so chances are they were still there when Amanda disappeared." Marlene waved across the restaurant at Joe Sajak, Ocean Vista's much sought after widower who, at four o'clock in the afternoon, had to be the earliest bird eating dinner in all of South Florida.

"What about the other boardsman, Sam Meyers? Do you think Jon Michael, Claude, and Roberto met him here after they'd returned from Acapulco?" Kate ripped the paper off her straw as Myrtle placed the ice cream soda in front of her.

"I know Sam Meyers," Myrtle said. "He brings his granny

here every Friday night for the fish fry. Ms. Meyers is an activist, you know, and a founding member of NOW. She's fighting city hall. The town fathers want to let some New York outfit buy the Rainbow Beach trailer park and tear it down to build yet another multimillion-dollar condo."

"I read about that," Kate said. "And I've driven past there many times on my way to Palm Beach. The only trailer park in the county directly on the ocean. It's been there for ages, right?"

Myrtle nodded. "Almost sixty years, and some of them folks are the original owners. Damn shame what's done in the name of progress. Anyway, Sam works with computers. Nice young man, not like that white trash, Claude Jensen, he hangs out with. That boy's been in and out of one correctional institution or another since he was thirteen. The state of Florida should build Claude his own wing. He's waiting trial for a DWI right now."

Good God. Kate wondered if Katharine's surfing lesson was over. "Myrtle, do you know Jon Michael Tyler too?"

"In a manner of speaking, I do. Hold the thought. The counterman's waving me over. I'll be back with those muffins in a sec, hon." Her pink and gray uniform stretched tight across her fanny as she hustled toward the counter.

Marlene arched her perfectly penciled-in left brow. "Myrtle's probably one of Jon Michael's grandmother's talking skull's clients." Her tone combined amusement and disdain.

Kate figured that Marlene, a woman who'd consulted fortune tellers, astrologists, and tarot card readers, shouldn't scoff at talking skulls. As she'd done so many times for more than sixty years, Kate kept her opinion to herself. "I'm really worried about Katharine, Marlene. Will you keep an eye on her tomorrow? I have to go to Jane's funeral up in Palm Beach."

"Oh, yeah, that stewardess who married a multimillionaire, just like the heroine of an old movie. I always wanted to be Doris Day, but who knew about Rock Hudson?" Marlene sighed. "Of course I'll watch our girl, Kate. The more I hear about these surfers the more I think Katharine's in over her head." Her sister-in-law's water metaphor made Kate even more nervous.

"Here we go." Myrtle placed two blueberry muffins the size of melons on the table. Kate shuddered at the calorie count, but figured she wouldn't eat at the picnic. Skipping dinner was one of the few perks of life without Charlie.

"So, what about Jon Michael?" Marlene asked Myrtle the question before Kate could. That happened a lot.

"Well, I'm a client of Florita Flannigan, his grandmother."

Marlene managed to kick Kate under the table while taking a bite of her muffin.

"The skull and I were old souls together. Romped through the Renaissance." Myrtle tapped her index finger against her double chin. "You two girls should make an appointment. There's always a real long wait to meet Mandrake, but me being so close to the family, I'm sure I could get you in. Maybe next week."

"Why don't you do that, Myrtle?" Kate said. "And as soon as possible. I really want to meet Florita Flannigan."

"I understand Jon Michael's a friend of Claude's," Marlene said.

"Right," Myrtle said. "All four of them surf together. Like I say, Sam's a good guy. And that Roberto's a charmer. I think Jon Michael's a sweet kid, but the skull has revealed to me and Florita that her grandson is courting disaster. I figure it must be connected to some scheme of Claude's."

Courting disaster. And courting Katharine? Kate shoved the muffin away.

Nine

Marlene hadn't had any time alone with Katharine. She worried about what the girl knew and how she'd gotten her information. Of Marlene's many past peccadilloes, the one she *absolutely* never wanted Kate to ever hear about was that four-martini fling with Charlie. As she stirred green peppers into her macaroni salad, she plotted how she could get Katharine alone and question her. Delicately, of course. Hah. When had she ever been delicate either in appearance or approach?

Because of the unpleasantness—Mary Frances's euphemism for the murder on the beach—during last year's Halloween costume party in the recreation room, this year the Ocean Vista board of directors had voted unanimously for a pre-Halloween picnic supper.

New Yorkers never referred to a meal served at the dinner hour as supper. Supper was a light meal served in a club like the Copacabana or a dance club after the theater, around eleven p.m.

No question, Marlene had compromised her principles living among all these Midwesterners and Southerners.

Sighing, she added chopped celery and deviled eggs as she glanced at the clock: 6:10. She had twenty minutes to fix her face and change her clothes. She wondered if the newly widowed Bernie Gordon from the eighth floor would be at the picnic. Maybe she'd wear her new scarlet harem pants. Go as a concubine. But where the hell had she put her off-the-shoulder black satin blouse? Though she'd gotten rid of most her treasures—well, okay, *junk*—at the Palmetto Beach mile-square flea market, followed by all of her furniture after last summer's back-to-back hurricanes, over the past month, Marlene had restored chaos to her apartment.

The condo's decorating committee had done a great job. The wooden picnic tables in the sand, courtesy of the city of Palmetto Beach, were covered with orange tablecloths featuring black cats and witches on broomsticks. Paper plates, strong enough to hold hot food, were decorated with ghosts and goblins. Orange and black balloons and jack-o'-lanterns were hanging on the fence around the pool area. All of the condo owners had brought their beach chairs and their favorite dishes.

Charcoal in the barbeque pit—also courtesy of the city—glowed, as Mary Frances, dressed as a very sexy, not at all scary witch, stirred a cauldron, actually an expensive copper pot from Williams-Sonoma, filled with meatballs in red sauce.

Joe Sajak served as the dancing ex-nun's sous chef, handing Mary Frances a huge spoon, saying, "The better to stir with, my dear." God, he was enough to make Marlene barf.

A breeze from the teal blue ocean ruffled the palm trees.

The sun hovered on the horizon. The clean, crisp scent from the sea proved as intoxicating as Marlene's double gin with a splash of tonic. Paradise found, Marlene thought, then rejected her cynical attitude. It was indeed a perfect evening. And she could *almost* understand why some Ocean Vista residents believed they lived in paradise.

No sign of Kate, who would be bringing the chocolate fudge cake she'd purchased at Dinah's. Her sister-in-law wasn't much of a baker or a cook. Somehow that deficiency—Kate had so damn few—pleased Marlene.

No sign of Katharine either. Or the surfers. Why? Those waves were as good as they get in South Florida.

Kate, in no mood for a picnic, watched the action on the beach through her picture window. The picnickers must be roasting in those costumes. Why did so many bright, seemingly sane, retirees revert to their second childhoods every Halloween?

She didn't dare step out onto the balcony where Marlene might spot her and wave her down. Katharine hadn't come home. Could a surfing lesson last for more than three hours? Kate didn't think so.

Restless, she picked up the *Sun-Sentinel* and read, for the third time, a follow-up story on Amanda Rowling's disappearance in Acapulco.

The girl's mother, Grace Rowling, was on her way to Fort Lauderdale. The Mexican police had advised Mrs. Rowling that the two surfers who'd been seen with her daughter on the night she'd vanished had returned to South Florida. Mrs. Rowling had an appointment with one of the surfers, but declined to give his name. The accompanying photographs of mother and daughter seemed eerily alike. Both appeared to be blonde, pretty, and far too wholesome to be part of such a sad story. Only the terror in Grace Rowling's eyes revealed the tragic truth.

Kate heard a key turn in the front door and stepped away from the window. A barking Ballou ran through the foyer.

"I thought I heard my favorite Westie." A smiling Katharine had returned.

The little dog yelped with abandon, delighted to see Katharine, his tail wagging, his tongue licking her hand.

"Hi, Nana. Aren't you going to the picnic?" Kate's granddaughter was flushed. Katharine's freckles seemed to have merged into one big rash. Sunburn or passion? Maybe a bit of both. Her red hair was wet and strewn with seaweed. The towel wrapped around her bikini was streaked and stained. Whatever Katharine had been doing had taken its toil.

"Do you want to go?" Kate asked, wondering if the girl had been drinking.

Katharine grinned. "Sure." For a brief moment, she looked and sounded almost like the girl Kate had known, before this angry young woman had emerged.

She turned and headed down the corridor toward the guest bathroom. "I want to grab a fast shower."

"Great," Kate said. "I'll bring the chocolate cake down and wait for you on the beach."

"Listen, Nana," Katharine called over her shoulder. "I've invited Jon Michael and his grandmother to the picnic. I hope that's okay."

Kate wondered if Florita Flannigan would bring the talking skull.

Ten

Kate, her mind in a jumble, crossed the pool area, holding Ballou's leash and his pooper-scooper with her right hand and the cake box in her left. Her appearance at the picnic would be delayed; the Westie needed a walk. So did his mistress.

She placed the box on the picnic table, said hi to Marlene, and then headed for the damp sand at the water's edge. She loved the sea, always had, even as a child more than half a century ago at Rockaway Beach where Queens meets the Atlantic Ocean. The sound of waves rolling in soothed her.

Early evening in October might be the best time of the year to walk along the shore in South Florida. The sky seemed to spring from the sea and stretch to the heavens, the sun a sinking semicircle, a pale moon waiting in the wings.

While the sharp salt air had cleared her head, her heart still hurt. What could she do to help Katharine? The answer was as sharp as the air: nothing. A young woman in the throes of her first real crush didn't desire advice to the lovelorn from her grandmother.

"Hey, Kate, wait up." Joe Sajak's voice broke into her reverie.

She hadn't heard his footsteps in the sand. Turning as Ballou tugged her forward, she said, "Oh hi, Joe," hoping he'd note her lack of enthusiasm. Ballou had expressed his feelings with a low growl.

Joe hadn't yet donned his Batman costume; maybe he was saving that for dessert.

"I need to talk to you." He grinned, showing teeth, bleached to bright white. The widower of Stella Sajak, who was murdered on the beach last Halloween, Joe had moved from grief to lust less than a week after his wife's funeral. Lean, with thick white hair, and the recipient of Stella's cash and condo, he fancied himself quite the catch. Several Ocean Vista widows, divorcees, and one ex-nun had fueled that fancy.

Kate gauged how rude her response should be. Would "sorry, I'm thinking" pass muster?

"It's about my love life."

Damn. In this game, she who hesitated lost. Kate stared at him, saying nothing, but wishing that Ballou who was toying with a dead fish would poop on Joe's toes.

"I've been playing the merry widower way too long." He sighed, then brushed a strand of expensively styled hair out of his Paul Newman blue eyes.

Kate, cursing silently, nodded. Where was he going with this?

"It's time for me to settle down, to stop flitting around, to get serious, and make one of my many lady friends very happy."

Ballou yelped, straining on his leash. Kate wanted to yelp too. Instead, she choked out, "Really?"

"Yes," Joe shouted. "I want to go steady, possibly get engaged, maybe even get married again. I've narrowed the field down to two and, though I've dated women from Miami to Palm Beach, the lucky ladies are both Ocean Vista residents." He leered at Kate.

Good God, she'd never dated him, never even brought him a casserole, so she couldn't be a candidate, could she?

"They're two very different women. One might say at either end of the morality yardstick." Joe paused, watching the waves, seeming to be deep in thought.

Since shallow Sajak had never expressed any depth before this moment, Kate figured his silent stare was for her benefit; no doubt he believed it added gravitas.

"Who?" Kate stammered, hating herself for asking, but hell, she had to end this conversation and get back to the picnic. Katharine must be there by now.

"Mary Frances, beautiful inside and out, but she's a virgin and a man has his needs. Dare I ask a nun to break her vow of chastity?"

Kate laughed so loud, Joe jumped.

"I don't see what's so damn funny, Kate."

She bit her lip. It was her turn to stare at the sea.

"My runner-up would be Marlene." Joe sounded solemn. "But I suspect she's been around the block, that she's slept with far too many men...three husbands for starters."

Knowing Marlene once had a crush on Joe—she'd had a crush on almost every man she'd ever met—but now couldn't stand him, Kate said, "Right. Her husbands were only the hors d'oeuvres."

With perfect timing, Ballou did his business. Kate used

the pooper-scooper, regretting that he'd missed Joe's left foot by less than an inch. She pulled on the little dog's leash. "Come on, Ballou. We're finished here."

Claude Jensen, perched high in his lifeguard seat, waved as she walked by. "Keep your dog outta the water, ma'am. Them sharks they saw up in Boca might be down here by now. One bite and that little hair ball's gone."

Marlene, emboldened by two gin and tonics, spotted Katharine, dressed as Britney Spears, all bare midriff and shoulders, and decided to ask the girl just exactly what she knew about her Auntie Marlene's checkered past before Kate and Ballou returned from their walk.

It took Marlene a few minutes to navigate around the three-deep crowd at the picnic table. By the time she reached Katharine, the girl had company: Jon Michael and an attractive older woman whom Marlene presumed was his grandmother.

The shoeless surfer wore white cutoff shorts and a purple hibiscus lei around his neck. His bare chest glistened as if he'd smothered it in grease. He smelled like lanolin, baby oil, and tea—one of Marlene's own favorite homemade tanning lotions—flowers, and pot. After fifty years, Marlene still recognized the aroma of marijuana.

"Auntie Marlene, you've already met Jon Michael." Katharine, her voice brimming with pride, turned toward the older woman. "And this is his grandmother, the famous Florita Flannigan."

Florita's flowers were on her head, a crown of lilies almost as white as her thick, well-styled, chin-length hair. A slim woman, her lightly tanned, heart-shaped face was sweet, albeit lined. She'd dressed in a white peasant blouse with a rose-colored drawstring and a ruffled rose ankle-length skirt. She was barefoot; her toenail polish matched her skirt. Marlene felt certain this wasn't a costume, that Florita had worn her work clothes.

Marlene extended her hand. "Welcome to Ocean Vista, Florita. Happy Halloween. Did you bring the skull?" Florita laughed, a tinkling laugh, like a schoolgirl's. "No, he doesn't make house calls."

Marlene liked her, but curbed her enthusiasm; the woman was, after all, Jon Michael's grandmother.

"We like Katharine very much." Florita's blue eyes sparkled.

Marlene figured that hadn't been a royal *we,* that Florita had been referring to herself and her grandson...and maybe to the talking skull. Had Katharine made his acquaintance?

"Can I make an appointment?" Marlene asked, hearing a hint of desperation in her voice. Meeting Jon Michael's grandmother's skull could lead to all kinds of inside information about the surfer. Kate would be so jealous.

Florita whipped a small spiral notebook out of her pocket and flipped it open. "You're in luck, Marlene. Our ten o'clock tomorrow morning canceled." Florita smiled. "Joe Sajak's next in line. He's been waiting for an appointment for weeks; I thought I'd surprise him tonight with this cancellation. They're so rare, you know. The lady who canceled has been arrested. I know Mandrake's advice could have prevented that unpleasantness. Anyway, Marlene, since you're Katharine's kin, you can have the appointment." Florita smiled again. "It's two hundred dollars for the hour."

Humph. Up from fifty-five dollars just a few days ago, Marlene thought but said, "Great!"

"Got beer?" Jon Michael headed toward the bar.

Katharine yelled over her bare shoulder as she followed Jon Michael. "Auntie Marlene, I'll be back in a flash. I can't wait to hear what you plan to discuss with the skull."

Marlene felt a flash of panic. Could the skull—or Florita Flannigan—have revealed her secrets to Katharine?

Eleven

Kate sipped a wine cooler that tasted like sour grapes. Or maybe Katharine's costume had turned her stomach. She dumped the wine in the sand and reached into her pocket for a Pepcid AC.

When would she hear from Nick? She'd left a detailed message asking the detective to check out Jon Michael Tyler and Roberto Romero, then for good measure, had thrown in Claude Jensen and Sam Meyers, even though she hadn't met Sam yet and knew almost nothing about him, other than that he, too, had a grandmother.

Jon Michael's grandmother, Florita Flannigan, was holding court under a palm tree in the pool area. Several Ocean Vista residents were her clients and devoted fans of the talking skull.

Down at the shoreline, Katharine and Jon Michael strolled arm in arm.

Kate stood, gulped, and headed toward the pool area.

Gassy or not, she needed to have a word with Mrs. Flannigan, who, Kate figured, must be Jon Michael's maternal grandmother. Where were his parents?

Florita sat in a blue and white plastic armchair at a round, glass table near the deep end of the pool. With all the chairs taken, some of the more agile Ocean Vista residents were sitting, legs dangling, on the diving board. Others stood, almost reverentially, waiting to catch Florita's eye. God, only in South Florida, Kate thought, but then she remembered how much a grilled cheese sandwich depicting the "face of the Virgin Mary" had sold for on eBay.

As Kate vied with Joe Sajak for Florita's attention, Katharine and Jon Michael returned from the ocean and sat on their heels near his grandmother's table. Ah, youth. Kate knew too well the spasms her back would have to weather if she even tried to get into a position like that. A few minutes later, Mary Frances arrived and, to Kate's annoyance, managed to fold herself down on her heels, establishing squatter's rights between Jon Michael and his grandmother.

Ex-nuns don't sweat, but Mary Frances certainly glowed. Tossing her long red hair, she broke into the conversation, interrupting Florita who was quoting the skull's position on recent world politics.

"Guess what?" Mary Frances asked, addressing no one, yet everyone. "I spent two hours this afternoon at the elimination round for this year's Broward County dance contest. Much to my surprise, Roberto Romero and I will be partners in the couples' competition for tango champions. We danced like Ginger and Fred in *Flying Down to Rio*." She sighed. "It's as if we were fated to dance together."

"Just how did you and that surfer get together?" Joe Sajak sounded like a man in pain.

"Fate, blessed fate. We both drew the same number."

"Hey, Mary Frances, I thought you already were Broward County's reigning tango queen," a short, chubby lady, who lived in the north wing, said.

"I am, indeed." Mary Frances smiled. "But this year they'll be choosing a king and a queen. A royal couple. Roberto's considered the best Latin dancer in Broward. Maybe Dade too." Balancing on one hand, she used the other to push stray curls out of her eyes. The wind had picked up. "His posture alone will make him a winner. Will make us both winners." Mary Frances sounded coy.

Kate's stomach jumped. Damn. Did she have another Pepcid AC in one of her pockets? What a hypocrite Mary Frances was, tangoing with the enemy. She deserved Joe Sajak...if he didn't die first of apoplexy.

"Look," the lady from the north wing shouted, pointing toward the beach. "The lifeguard just raised the shark-warning flag."

The antique mahogany grandmother clock in the foyer—one of Charlie's prized possessions that he'd insisted on moving down from Rockville Centre, though it didn't go with anything in the off-white and beige condo that Edmund, their son Peter's partner, had decorated—chimed eleven times. Kate sat wide awake on the balcony, sipping decaf tea and wondering where her granddaughter was.

A spurt of anger, red and hot, shot through Kate. She'd be damned if she reined her granddaughter in, and damned if she didn't.

How would Charlie have handled Katharine's metamorphosis? Even that world-weary, yet surprisingly optimistic New York City homicide detective might have been stumped.

Debating whether or not to have another cup of tea, Kate stood, disturbing the Westie who'd been dozing by her side. "Sorry, Ballou. We should both be in bed." The difference between *should* and *could* never seemed clearer.

Exhausted, knowing she had to drive up to Palm Beach for Jane's funeral in the morning, she *couldn't* force herself to go to bed.

The moon hung like a huge ball of burnished gold, lighting up the sky. Kate crossed to the railing and looked north toward Fort Lauderdale. Sure enough, Katharine and Jon Michael were on the beach. Had she heard them before she saw them? No matter, their voices were raised now, not loud enough for Kate to make out the words, but the tone sounded angry. It appeared as if they were quarreling, Katharine gesturing like the New Yorker she was.

Kate, in her nightgown, wondered if she should get dressed and go down and drag her grandchild off the beach. Instead, she waited and watched, praying Katharine wouldn't venture into an ocean on shark alert. If her granddaughter stuck as much as a toe in the water, Kate would scream.

Jon Michael staggered. His *goddamn* reached the balcony loud and clear. Had Katharine shoved him? Recovering his balance, he grabbed his surfboard and ran into the ocean. Kate watched him ride a wave until he became a tiny speck on the horizon and then disappeared.

Once again, Kate wondered why Jon Michael surfed in the dark. And where was Roberto tonight?

When she glanced back at the beach, there was no sign of Katharine.

Kate decided to go to bed; she couldn't deal with her

granddaughter now. And as Scarlett O'Hara said, tomorrow was another day.

A few minutes later, Kate heard Katharine come in. She thought the girl might be crying.

Damn. Damn. Damn.

Kate closed her eyes as the clock chimed midnight.

Twelve

Monday morning, October 30

The skull resided with his owner in a pink bungalow with a white picket fence. A calligraphy-scripted shingle, hanging on a lamppost in the well-tended yard, read TANNING SALON & SPIRITUAL COUNSELING.

Marlene had spent the morning on the internet researching the skull's history and success story or, maybe more accurately, Florita Flannigan's success story.

Forty years ago, Florita, a native of Rhode Island, had fled to Florida as a young divorcee to escape New England's "wicked winters and rigid morality," and settled in Palmetto Beach, then a small fishing village, to raise her toddler as a "sea nymph." When the nymph turned nineteen she'd fled Palmetto Beach, leaving behind her two-year-old son, Jon Michael, to be raised by his grandmother.

While divorcing her third husband—a gal Marlene could relate to—Florita enrolled in beauty school, graduated with honors, then opened a beauty shop in her front parlor.

When Florita had discovered that Floridians, surrounded by sunshine, would pay big money for artificial rays' instant gratification, she turned her beauty shop into Palmetto Beach's first tanning salon. The operation was an overnight success. Raising Jon Michael had proved more difficult. Still, from Florita's profile in *Parade* magazine, Marlene gathered the grandmother and grandson had a close, if often contentious, relationship.

For the crystal skull and Florita, it had been love at first sight They'd met in Mexico. An East Indian mystic, who owned a souvenir store in Acapulco—Marlene found it odd how Acapulco kept popping up and even odder how an East Indian had been living there—swore that the skull he'd found in an Incan temple's ruins had magical powers to heal both body and soul. Florita, entranced with the four-thousand-year-old skull's mesmerizing features, had paid the East Indian mystic one dollar for every year the skull had been around. She named him Mandrake, after the magician in her favorite comic strip.

Parade had quoted Florita: "I figured buying a healing relic with a proven history of curing folks for four thousand dollars was a real bargain."

The article pointed out that the skull, one of several traveling the New Age circuit, didn't actually talk; he communicated via telepathy. Some believers heard more during their private sessions than others. And Florita often acted as interpreter. The photo, credited to Jon Michael Tyler, showed a twenty-pound piece of crystal, crafted to look like a human skull, complete with sunken eye sockets and missing teeth.

True believers, including Donald Trump's butler and a former First Lady, who'd met with several of the world's best-known talking skulls, testified that Mandrake was the most impressive, citing conversations ranging from clairvoyant to miraculous.

One self-proclaimed psychic from Cincinnati had reported that Florita's skull had acted as a medium, translating a message in Romanian from an ancestor on her mother's side who'd been a warlock during the Middle Ages.

Marlene had absorbed all this information with no prejudice and concluded that Florita was a con artist, her clients were crazy, and her grandson was a snake.

She pushed open the white, wooden gate, walked up the primrose-lined path, and rang the doorbell. It chimed to the tune of "What Kind of Fool Am I?"

Florita's smile seemed forced and, though she wore a pretty caftan with long, flowing sleeves, her hair lacked last evening's perfection and her face was drawn and wan. "Do come in, Marlene. I'm so glad to see you." She sounded anything but.

The South Florida bungalow, furnished like a New England cottage, oozed cozy charm. Cabbage roses and chintz abounded. A carafe of tea and a plate of oatmeal cookies were on a small mahogany table in front of a pink and lime green plaid loveseat.

Florita gestured toward the loveseat. "Please sit down, Marlene. Mandrake and I have had a difficult morning."

Marlene sat. The cookies looked homemade.

"It pains me when he gets upset over my problems." Florita, a perfect hostess, held out the plate. Marlene took two cookies and said nothing, just waited, a trick she'd learned from Kate.

"We both sense disaster." Florita's hand shook as she poured the tea. She fussed a bit, passing sugar and milk, and then sat on a cabbage rose-covered club chair catty-corner to the loveseat.

Marlene sipped in silence, still waiting.

"Jon Michael didn't come home last night." A tear rolled down his grandmother's cheek.

"Well, that's not so unusual for a boy his age, is it?" Marlene worked to put warmth and empathy into her voice.

"Well, as Mandrake pointed out, Jon Michael always calls when he's not coming home." She gave Marlene a sly smirk. "I withhold his allowance when he doesn't."

"Allowance? Just how old is he, anyway?" Damn. She'd blown her fake concern with a blast of sharp criticism.

"He'll be twenty-one on Halloween." Florita fiddled with a huge diamond ring on her right hand. It sparkled in the sunlight and Marlene figured it had be at least ten carats. "I assure you my grandson earns his allowance, Marlene. Jon Michael does a great deal of promotional work for Mandrake and me."

"Well, that's wonderful." Her words were warmer than the tea. Marlene felt relieved. She knew Katharine *had* come home; she'd spotted her this morning.

"It's just that..." Florita began, and then paused. Marlene considered patting her hostess's hand, but settled for an encouraging nod.

"I don't like my grandson hanging out with those lowlife surfers. I keep telling him they're not our sort of people." Anger distorted Florita's features. "Especially Claude Jensen. The boy comes from a long line of white trash. The father's a sociopath, serving a life sentence; he killed a girl in Dade. Claude's a regular chip off the old block. He's served time in jail too, and he's awaiting trial now. Mandrake and I believe

Claude's leading Jon Michael astray. Sam Meyers seems okay, but why he's hanging out with the surfers is a mystery to me. What's in it for him?" Marlene found herself believing Florita. But then she remembered that telling great stories was how cons sucked their marks in.

The owner of the best tanning salon and skull-reading operation in South Florida frowned. "There's another serious concern, Marlene."

What now? Marlene placed her now tepid tea on the table and met Florita's eyes. They'd turned cold.

"Mandrake says you're not a true believer. He doesn't wish to meet you." Florita stood. "There'll be no charge for today's visit. No hard feelings. I'll pack up the rest of these cookies for you."

Marlene was about to tell her what she could do with her cookies when Florita shoved aside her flowing sleeve to glance at her watch. A diamond bracelet Rolex.

Hot damn! Could Florita be Diamond Lil?

Thirteen

Monday evening, October 30

The body floating face down in the water was a blond. Kate felt faint, but there was nothing to grab except Marlene. Before she could reach out, Kate felt Marlene's strong arm, the arm of a former champion swimmer, encircle her, enabling her to keep her balance, to stay on her feet.

The bearded young man in the rowboat covered the bloody stump with a tarp as the slim fisherman jumped into the water and swam toward the body.

The heavy set fisherman on the pier had reached 911. Help was on its way, but Kate knew no one could help. Dear God, which blond surfer lay dead in the water? Claude or Jon Michael? Or someone else?

Like a television promo, a picture of Katharine quarreling with Jon Michael on the beach late last night flashed through Kate's head, followed by a dull ache. What had happened to the surfer—and the dead man might well be a total stranger—was an accident. A shark attack. Too often Kate's imagination could be macabre, painful, and off-kilter. Still, she felt unnerved and, yes, frightened.

The slim fisherman had the body in tow. "Give me a hand," he yelled to the young man in the rowboat.

As the men struggled to get the body over the side of the boat, the ambulance's siren heralded its approach, and Kate caught a glimpse of Jon Michael's profile.

She slipped out of Marlene's grip and slumped down on the dock, scraping her palm. The last thing she saw before she started to scream was the one-legged corpse landing in the boat.

"A little drink never hurt anyone." Marlene handed a gin and tonic in a tall, frosted glass, garnished with lime, to her sister-in-law. "Consider it medicinal."

They were sitting in Kate's living room, so beige and so bland, with nothing out of place, wondering where Katharine had gone and how they would tell her Jon Michael was dead.

Was this what shell-shock felt like? Kate reached for the drink. Her hand shook, but she drained a quarter of the glass in one gulp. It didn't wash away the scene on the pier.

A paramedic had pronounced Jon Michael dead. No one covered his body. A police officer briefly interviewed Kate, Marlene, and the three fishermen, and then told them to leave, that someone would be in touch with them later. Nick Carbone? Why hadn't he called her back? She'd stared out at the ocean, never once glancing down at Jon Michael's body or that bloody stump. Another policeman held the piece of surfboard as if it were made of platinum. Maybe to cops, all clues were platinum.

Kate finished the gin and tonic and considered having another.

She'd never thought she could feel resentful about her granddaughter's actions. But Nana's condo had made Katharine's desperate pursuit of Jon Michael both convenient and affordable. Her darling Katharine had been using Kate. No question she'd wanted the surfer at any cost.

What had happened to her granddaughter in Acapulco? Had she been wooed, then dumped? Had passion trumped pride? Why else would Katharine have followed Jon Michael to Palmetto Beach? And what had they been arguing about on the beach just before the surfer rode his last wave?

"You ready for a refill?" Marlene tapped Kate's empty glass.

"Sure. Why not?" Kate used her napkin to wipe the sweat from her forehead. Sweating in air-conditioning. Not good. She fought an urge to scream. "Marlene, did Katharine say anything to you when you saw her walking Ballou this morning?"

Kate watched Marlene, standing behind the small rattan bar near the dining room, pour a dollop of tonic into the gin, then stir. She considered telling her sister-in-law to add more tonic, then figured, what the hell, getting a bit tipsy might not be a bad idea right now.

"Katharine waved, said hi, but nothing else. Why?" Marlene put the drink on the table in front of Kate. "I was on my way to visit Florita. My mind was on Mandrake."

"I'm wondering—well, worrying—about where the devil Katharine could be. It's almost eight and no one has seen her since early this morning."

"Yeah," Marlene agreed, not offering any ideas.

Kate shook her head, forcing herself to concentrate on

something else. "So, you're convinced Florita cons her clients and doesn't really believe the skull can communicate."

"Hell yes. The Golden Glow tanning salon's legit, but the talking skull's a con game. Florita wouldn't let me see him perform because she damn well knew I was on to her." Marlene waved a bottle of vermouth over her second dry martini.

The intercom rang. Kate, hoping it might be Katharine, ran into the foyer to answer.

"You have a visitor, Mrs. Kennedy." Miss Mitford sounded even more somber than usual. "A Mrs. Rowling is here in the lobby. She'd like to see you."

"Mrs. Rowling?" Kate said. "I don't think I know…"

"Amanda Rowling, that girl who disappeared in Acapulco," Marlene shouted from the bar. "Grace Rowling's her mother!"

A shaking Kate said in a strained voice, "Please send Mrs. Rowling up, Miss Mitford."

Marlene downed half her martini in one gulp. "She must know about Katharine and Jon Michael. Why else would she come?" Marlene sounded as nervous as Kate felt.

"Maybe she thinks I know something." Icy fear ran through Kate's body, drying the sweat leaving her weak. What did the woman want? Had she heard about the surfer's death? Or, God forbid, could Grace Rowling be bringing bad news about Katharine?

Fourteen

The sharp rap on the door made Kate jump and Ballou bark. She willed herself to smile as she opened it.

Grace Rowling wore khakis and a white polo shirt; she had short blonde hair, big brown eyes in an oval face, and, though she had to be in her forties, was as small and slim as a teenager. She would be pretty if her features weren't etched in pain.

"Come in, Mrs. Rowling." Empathy replaced distrust as Kate shook the woman's hand. "We're very sorry about your daughter."

"Please call me Grace, Mrs. Kennedy."

"I will if you'll call me Kate." She pointed to the bar. "And this is my sister-in-law, Marlene Friedman."

"Would you like a drink?" Marlene asked.

"A Diet Coke, please."

"Should I put a shot of rum in it?"

Grace almost managed a smile. "Make it half a shot.

Thanks, Marlene." She petted Ballou, who was sniffing her feet. "I'm sorry to barge in on you like this, but I'm very concerned about your granddaughter, Katharine."

The icy fear settled in Kate's heart. She sputtered. "Why?"

"Those surfers, Kate." Grace Rowling sounded patient, as if she were explaining the obvious to a child. "They're dangerous men. I just heard that Jon Michael was attacked by a shark. Well, good. One down, two to go."

Grace's hard words—she spoke so softly and sounded so Midwest wholesome—had caught Kate off guard. "Two to go?" she asked, grateful that Marlene had remained quiet.

"Yes. Claude and Roberto. They were with Jon Michael and my daughter the night Amanda disappeared." Grace blinked, but tears fell and then rolled down her cheeks. She didn't wipe them away. Kate doubted she even noticed them.

For a moment Kate wondered if Grace Rowling had anything to do with Jon Michael's death. How? Had she hired someone to sic a shark on him? Kate felt as crazy as her thoughts.

"I've seen you on television, Grace," Marlene said, "and it's all so sad. Why don't you tell us what you think happened to Amanda?"

Sometimes Marlene really got it right. Kate smiled at her sister-in-law.

Grace smiled at Marlene too. Clearly, she'd come to tell them her story and she needed them to listen. "My daughter is beautiful and talented. She's only a fair student but a wonderful actress. She played Liza in *My Fair Lady* in the senior play. And she's so popular. Everyone loves Amanda."

It broke Kate's heart to hear Grace talk in the present tense. Did she really believe Amanda was still alive?

"Acapulco was her graduation present, her last fling with her two girlfriends before starting college. She's enrolled in UCLA, you know." Grace sipped her Diet Coke, probably laced with more rum than she'd wanted. "On the night before she was to fly home, my daughter, who'd told her girlfriends she had a date—but hadn't told them his name—left a club with a young, blond male. Several witnesses, including the bartender, swear to that."

"With just one of the boys?" Kate asked.

"Yes, though the bartender said she'd been drinking at the bar earlier with three young men, all surfers, two blonds and a Latino. They'd been in the bar before, but he didn't know their names."

"But he couldn't recall which blond?" Kate vaguely remembered hearing that during one of Grace Rowling's countless television interviews.

Grace tried to grin; it turned into a grimace. "I guess all tourists look alike to Mexican bartenders."

"So either Claude or Jon Michael left with Amanda." Marlene was mixing another martini.

Ballou had settled down between Kate and Grace, a compliment to their guest, and was now snoring.

"Well, the three surfers admitted they'd bought Amanda a drink, but swore that none of them left with her." Grace placed her right index finger on her left pinkie. "Claude says he never saw Amanda leave; he was in the men's room." She moved her tight index finger to her ring finger. "And Roberto and Jon Michael swear they'd left the club at the same time and saw Amanda heading toward the beach. Alone."

"What do the Mexican police think?" Kate asked, knowing the answer.

Grace groaned. "They claim they're still investigating all

leads, but they allowed those three surfers to leave the country after only asking them a few questions. 'Señora Rowling, it is all very suspicious, but there is no evidence and no body' has become their mantra."

"And Amanda had mentioned the surfers to you before she disappeared." Marlene drained her glass. Kate hoped it was Marlene's nightcap.

"Yes, we talked every night. Amanda told me on the phone the day before she disappeared that she had a crush on a sexy blond surfer." Grace sighed. "It had to be Jon Michael. No girl in her right mind would describe Claude Jensen as sexy. My daughter has made some poor choices in men, but she would never have gotten past yellow teeth and no brains."

Kate figured there might have been more than two blond surfers in Acapulco last summer, but only said, "How did you learn the surfers were in Palmetto Beach?"

"I hired a private detective. He's doing what the Mexican police should be doing, investigating those three men." Grace shook her head. "As for me, I'll haunt them. I'll follow them to the ends of the earth, at least until my money runs out." Her eyes filled with tears. "Those three bastards know where my daughter is." She wiped her eyes with a cocktail napkin.

Kate, always within reach of Pepcid AC, Kleenex, and Tylenol, dug into her handbag and handed Grace a small package of tissues.

"Thanks," Grace whispered as her face crumbled. "Amanda and I were very close. If she were alive, she'd call me. She's dead, isn't she?"

Neither Kate nor Marlene answered Grace's question.

"If Jon Michael killed Amanda, now he's dead and I'll never know the truth." Grace's agony was palpable. "Do you think someone killed him?"

Thinking Grace would be the prime suspect, Kate said, "No. I saw Jon Michael's body. I'm sure a shark killed him."

Grace shook her head. "Is your granddaughter here, Kate? I really need to talk to her."

Fifteen

Tuesday morning, October 31

The image of Jon Michael's bloody stump woke Kate up just before the clock struck seven. If only there was a delete button for the subconscious.

Ballou yelped as she crawled out of bed, nuzzling her ankle as she headed toward the bathroom. Kate had heard Katharine come in at eleven thirty and, though wide awake reading Ava Gardner's biography, she hadn't gotten up. She'd decided to wait until morning to discuss Jon Michael's death and Grace Rowling's visit. Now that morning had arrived, Kate dreaded the conversation, wondering if her granddaughter already knew about the surfer.

Tempted to go back to bed, instead she walked to the kitchen to make a cup of tea, her lifelong panacea.

Katharine sat at the kitchen table clutching her own cup of tea. Somehow that pleased Kate.

"Nana, Jon Michael's dead. Did you know that?"

Kate heard the heartbreak in Katharine's voice, almost a replay of Grace Rowling's tone last night.

"I'm so sorry, darling." Kate put her arms around her granddaughter, not sure what else to say. She gave Katharine a long hug, and then turned on the jet under the kettle.

"Claude called me." The girl had dark circles under puffy eyes. She'd been crying long and hard. "Attacked by a shark. What a terrible way to die. I cried all night. Your couch must be totally tearstained."

"You didn't sleep in the guest room?"

"Mom's in the guest room." Katharine didn't hide her disgust.

"Jennifer's here?" Kate reeled, feeling out of control.

"Yeah, she sure is. She flew down on Sunday night and checked into the Boca Raton Hotel, you know, that resort on the beach; nothing but the best for Mom, right?" Katharine screwed up her nose, reminding Kate of Charlie's expression of disgust. No doubt Jennifer had checked out of the hotel and slept here last night. She hadn't wanted to let Katharine out of her sight.

"Mom said she had an appointment with a client up in Palm Beach yesterday morning, but I know she's been spying on me, Nana. Now she's insisting I go home with her today. But I'm not going. Not today. Not ever. I promised Jon Michael's grandmother when I called her this morning that I'd be at his funeral and no one, not even Jennifer Lowell Kennedy, can stop me."

So Katharine had spoken to Florita Flannigan, who Marlene had suspected might be Diamond Lil, bank robber extraordinaire. What had the girl been up to yesterday? And why had Grace Rowling wanted to talk to her? Grace had declined to tell Kate, only saying she needed to speak to Katharine alone and she'd be back.

Confused and overwhelmed, Kate tried to keep it simple.

"I heard you come in last night," she said as the kettle whistled. She poured the boiling water into her cup, and then jiggled the tea bag as if that would make the tea brew faster. "But I didn't hear your mother."

"No reason you should have, Nana. We weren't talking and Mom went straight to bed." Her granddaughter sounded drained, but much more like her old self, the hard edge gone.

Kate stuck a bagel in the toaster, though she wasn't sure she could eat, then faced Katharine. "Marlene and I were worried last night. We wondered where you'd been all day."

Katharine stared at the tile floor, beige and bland like almost everything else in the condo. Less is more, Edmund, her son Peter's partner, had assured her. One day she'd paint the kitchen walls red, but for now she waited, sensing Katharine might open up.

"I'm sorry, Nana. I screwed up." She sounded as if she meant it; her eyes welled up with tears again. Katharine wiped her eyes and took a deep breath. "Life sucks."

Kate spread strawberry jam on the two halves of the toasted bagel and handed one to Katharine. "Yes, I guess right now it does. Have another cup of tea and we'll take Ballou for a walk on the beach. Maybe we can sort things out; then, if you'd like, we can go see Mrs. Flannigan later." If Kate had an ulterior motive, she didn't feel obliged to mention it.

"Cool. Let's get out of here before my mother wakes up."

In the glow of the morning light, the sun on their backs, its rays dappling the sand with golden streaks, and the Atlantic Ocean caressing their bare feet, Kate inhaled a brief moment of happiness; then Katharine spoke.

"I wanted to kill Jon Michael, Nana. That's why I'm so upset he's dead. Why I have to go to his funeral."

Trying to show no emotion, Kate asked, "Why? What did he do to you, darling?"

"He broke my heart and, worse, he made a fool of me." Katharine sighed. "No, that's not true. I was already a fool for loving him." She kicked a dead crab out of her path and into Ballou's. He eagerly explored the prize.

The sadness in her granddaughter's voice made Kate want to take the girl into her arms, but she had to hear this out.

"When I met him in Acapulco, he seemed so wonderful, so thoughtful. And so cool. Jon Michael made me laugh, tried to teach me to surf. I think I loved him from the moment I met him. But he didn't love me back. Not even in the beginning. And when I left Acapulco, he never said good-bye and never called me. Do you know how I found out he was in Palmetto Beach, Nana?"

Kate, afraid to say a word, afraid Katharine might shut down, just shook her head.

"From Amanda Rowling's mother on the *Today* show. Maybe I'm lucky I didn't disappear too. Amanda arrived in Acapulco like three days after I'd left."

"If Jon Michael hurt you so, why did you follow him here?" She tried to keep her tone neutral and calm, but a hint of fear had crept in.

"I loved him."

Kate had never heard three little words convey so much sadness.

The wind had picked up, heralding rain. In South Florida, no one got too excited about a sudden storm; it often ended as quickly as it arrived.

"Then Sunday night on the beach," Katharine met Kate's eyes, "were you watching us from the balcony, Nana?"

As rain began to pelt her back and Ballou barked, Kate gulped and said, "Yes."

"You witnessed our final scene." Spoken like the film student that Katharine was. Her red hair was soaked, strands of curls were plastered to her cheeks and flopping into her eyes. She didn't seem to notice. "His last words were, 'Take a hike, bitch.'"

Kate's cell phone rang. Thinking it might be Jennifer, she was surprised to see Nick Carbone's number.

"Hello." She sounded impatient and stressed, but she didn't care. She'd wondered why he hadn't called; now she had neither the time nor the inclination to speak to him. The relentless rain kept falling, drenching her baseball cap and sweat suit.

"Sorry I didn't get back to you sooner. I was down in Key Largo following up a lead. But I'm calling about Jon Michael Tyler's death. Another piece of his surfboard washed up on shore yesterday and the preliminary lab tests show some strange results. We're doing more tests and we're opening up a homicide investigation. I need to speak to Katharine."

Sixteen

Marlene glanced at the clock. It was 8:20. Damn. She rolled over, knowing she'd never get back to sleep.

Kate had called around eleven thirty last night to let her know Katharine had come home. So Marlene, relieved, had watched *Laura* until two thirty, glad she knew it by heart, because those three martinis had clouded her concentration. After she'd fallen asleep she kept waking up, almost every hour on the hour. Something had been nagging her. Something Florita Flannigan said about Sam Meyers, the fourth boardsman. The surfer they'd seen but never met. The only one, except for her grandson, Florita had seemed to respect. Maybe Sam would know why Roberto and Jon Michael went surfing at midnight. And, just maybe, Sam knew what had happened in Acapulco.

She bolted out of bed. Why not let Kate and Katharine have some time alone? Marlene was not often selfless, but hell, she had other plans for today anyway. Truth be told, she could use another day away from Katharine, who was depressed and depressing. Not to mention that any minute the girl might drop a bombshell about her Auntie Marlene's past. And a drive with the top down—of course, it would have to stop raining—might clear the cobwebs. Maybe last night she had downed four martinis, not three.

Marlene had always believed the difference between a drinker and a drunk was how they performed the morning after. To prove her theory, she'd dragged herself through some major-league hangovers. This one was minor.

She'd get herself dressed and head up to Palm Beach County to visit Sam in his granny's trailer. Granny Meyers couldn't be any less hospitable than Granny Flannigan, could she? Now what would Harriet Vane wear?

The sun came out as Marlene hit Deerfield Beach. Bright, beautiful, comforting. She put the white '57 Chevy's top down, then sang along with Tony Bennett and lit a Virginia Slim. Still sneaking cigarettes at sixty-eight, she'd gotten more grief for smoking at sixty-six than she had at sixteen. So, a three-pack-a-day smoker for over fifty years, she'd lied when she swore she'd quit. She'd cut back, but what she did in the privacy of her home and car was nobody's business.

She figured Kate knew the truth and had decided to ignore Marlene's dirty little habit as long as she didn't flaunt it. Kate had overlooked most of Marlene's faults for decades on end. A wave of guilt consumed her. Damn. Why hadn't she filled her flask? Hair of the dog would be good about now. She wondered if Granny Meyers might be a drinking woman.

As she crossed into Palm Beach County, the grass got greener and stood up straighter. The Boca Raton condo strip ranged from ornate to palatial. During the last four decades, some impressive and costly condominiums—the more French the name of the building, the more expensive its apartments—had been constructed along A1A in Boca. But that was BT. Before Trump. Some of his tower's apartments went for twenty-seven million dollars. A world gone mad, though this season, there was a glut of condos; it was becoming a buyers' market for the first time in years.

The light traffic in the one-lane road going north made the drive a breeze. She savored the ocean to her right and the mansions to her left as she approached her destination. To say a trailer park located on A1A in Palm Beach County, minutes from the city of Palm Beach, was an oddity would be an understatement of the greatest magnitude. For years, tourists traveling to the Breakers or Worth Avenue would pass through the tiny hamlet of Rainbow Beach and marvel at its trailer park abutting the Atlantic Ocean, and just minutes away from Mar-a-Lago, the former Marjorie Merriweather Post mansion, now also owned by the ubiquitous Trump.

Annette Meyers, a New York City transplant who'd lived in the Rainbow Beach trailer park for thirty-five years, wasn't about to let her home be destroyed without a fight. She'd rallied the other residents and, twenty-nine strong, the trailer owners filed a class action suit against the city of Rainbow Beach. The problem here, as with other inland trailer parks in Broward and Palm Beach Counties, was that the parks' residents owned their trailers, but not the land they were on. The city of Rainbow Beach owned the park and was executing its right of ownership. Six months ago, during a town meeting, Meyers had shouted the New York more graphic version of "horsefeathers," and then hired the aging but still blustery attorney H. Lee Daley.

Marlene and Kate wondered where Granny Meyers had gotten the money. H. Lee Daley didn't come cheap.

She turned right toward the sea into the quaint beach

colony, its pastel trailers equipped with white picket fences and tiny green lawns. No trailer trash here, just a spectacular ocean view and the best trailer park in the universe.

An elderly man—anyone who appeared to be five or more years older than Marlene qualified as elderly, though according to Medicare, so did she—tended a rose garden in front of his trailer, the first "house" on her left.

"Hi," she said, oozing charm. "Could you please tell me where Annette Meyers lives?"

"Who wants to know?" His gray eyes were wary and his body language indicated distrust and, maybe, disdain. She wished she'd worn something sexy, instead of the most tailored pantsuit she owned, but she'd wanted to be low key. She could hear Kate laughing at her for even entertaining the notion of appearing low key. And it wouldn't have made a difference if she were stark naked; this old guy wouldn't have even noticed.

"An old friend and a sister member of NOW," she lied.

"One of them, huh?" He pointed to the east. "Keep going. Ms. Meyers is in the first house off the beach on the left."

The trailer was pale aqua, the exact color of its owner's eyes, Marlene noted as she opened the door. Annette Meyers had broad shoulders, a robust body, and stood straight and tall, taller than Marlene, which put her at almost six feet. She wore her gray-streaked black hair like Gloria Steinem's, only shorter and sleeker. Her plaid shirt was well pressed and her jeans stretched over ample hips, though not nearly as ample as Marlene's. She was barefoot and her toenails were painted cherry red: a feminist with flare.

"Come in, come in, I've been expecting you." Granny Meyers's voice was as robust as her body.

Marlene, puzzled but pleased to be inside, looked around

the comfortable living/dining area. Charming. And its to-scale picture window had a view of the sea.

"You're a little early. Can I get you a cold drink?" Annette Meyers walked over to a small bar. "Beer or soda?" Like Marlene, she added an "r" to soda.

Since it was not yet eleven and she hated beer—a margarita might have been a different story—Marlene said, "Soda, please," and went back to wondering who the hell Annette thought she was.

Her hostess reached for a glass, and then peered at Marlene. "Aren't you a bit overdressed? We're forming a human chain on the ground; you might be dragged off to jail."

Seventeen

It occurred to Kate, and not for the first time, that her daughter-in-law Jennifer could be a prissy pain. On Jennifer's mother's side, the family line went back to John Adams and any history buff knew what a prig he'd been.

Kate, all too familiar with Nick Carbone's tactics and how he ran a murder investigation, had offered her best advice, but instead of listening, Jennifer was speed-dialing her attorney in New York.

The three generations of women sat in Kate's kitchen, their tea growing cold as they waited for the detective to arrive.

Katharine lost in a silence propelled by fear had said nothing since she'd heard Carbone wanted to question her. Ballou, his eyes closed, lay at the girl's feet.

And where had Marlene gone? Kate had tried both her home and cell phones. No answer. Maybe Marlene had forgotten to turn her cell on; that would be just like her, wouldn't it? Kate's impatience caught her attention: misplaced anger, Marlene wasn't the problem here.

The degree of Jennifer's distress was evident in her lack of grooming. She'd awakened to the news that her daughter was about to be questioned in a homicide investigation and hadn't even bothered to run a comb through her ash blonde hair. Her pale green eyes, minus shadow and mascara, appeared smaller and, without pencil extending them, her brows ended right after the arch.

The cool stockbroker, paid all those high commissions for her advice, had panicked and called her New York attorney for his.

"Mom," Katharine said, breaking her silence, "why won't you listen to Nana? She's dating the detective."

Katharine's presumptuous conclusion bandied about so cavalierly, and the resulting look of amazement on Jennifer's face was worth Kate's embarrassment. Even better, it worked. Jennifer said, "I'll get back to you, Henry," and hung up.

Kate drained the last of her tepid tea.

"Any suggestions, Kate?" Jennifer snapped, spilling her tea into the saucer.

Still fretting about where Katharine had been all day yesterday, Kate succumbed to an urge to throw her daughter-in-law off guard and said, "Nick might be interested in why—and when—you flew down to Fort Lauderdale, Jennifer."

A flushed Katharine fidgeted in her chair, then stood—disturbing Ballou, who yelped and moved over to Kate's foot—and put the kettle back on to boil.

Jennifer waved her right hand as if swatting a mosquito. "Where the hell are you coming from, Kate?"

Kate didn't have a clue, but not for a New York minute did she buy into Jennifer's story about meeting a client in Palm Beach. And neither would Nick. Like Katharine, Kate believed Jennifer had traveled from the city on a mission: to bring her daughter home. What lengths would Jennifer have gone to in order to achieve that goal? Kate laughed, nervous laughter. She really didn't think her daughter-in-law had anything to do with Jon Michael's death. It was a shark, wasn't it? And a shark attack couldn't be a homicide, could it?

"What's so damn funny, Kate?" Jennifer stood too, towering over Kate, her hands on hips, her body language shouting confrontation. "A detective—your boyfriend, I might add—is on his way to interrogate my daughter, and you've just accused me of God knows what, and now you're laughing."

Katharine stared down at the kitchen floor as if entranced with those vapid beige tiles.

The telephone rang, jarring the three women. Kate rose and answered it, saying, "Hello," in a shaky voice.

"It's Nick, Kate." Self-assured. Not the least bit shaky. "This Tyler investigation is mushrooming. I'd prefer Katharine come to my office." He hesitated, then added, "Can you be here at twelve thirty?" Phrased as a request, but more like a command.

"We'll be there," Kate said, then hung up, and whirled around to face her daughter-in-law and granddaughter. "Get dressed, Jennifer. Katharine's due at the police station in an hour." She glanced at the uneaten bagels. "We should try to eat something. And if we don't want to be late we need to leave here by noon. It's almost the off-season and the bridge is up more than it's down."

Jennifer bit her lip. "Does Katharine need an alibi?"

"Why, are you thinking about lying to protect me, Mom? Or would providing me with an alibi cover both our butts?"

Kate sighed. It should be a fun ride across the Neptune Boulevard Bridge to Palmetto Beach Police headquarters.

Eighteen

Be careful what you lie about, Marlene thought, or your scenario might come true and bite you in the behind.

Annette, the aging hippie, had planned a sit-in and, believing Marlene to be one of the NOW volunteers, expected her to lie down with all—well, most of the other trailer owners, a few had balked—to demonstrate civil disobedience and to be willing to go to jail for their cause.

"You mean the demolition crew is arriving today?" Marlene asked, thinking of the old man tending his garden. No wonder he seemed so cranky.

"Indeed. And none of the owners will leave. Even the most conservative among us, who refuse to actively engage in passive resistance, are holding firm. Didn't Beth explain all this to you? And where are the other women? Beth promised support from our local chapter. One person hardly qualifies as support." Annette put on her glasses and peered at Marlene. "Funny, I've never seen you at any of our meetings."

"I'm from the Fort Lauderdale chapter." Marlene, lying

yet again, hoped there was one. "You know, Annette, maybe I'll have that beer."

"There you go." She reached into the tiny refrigerator and handed Marlene a beer. "And there's marijuana around here somewhere. Now where did I stash it? We deserve a toke today; that's my motto." Her hostess bustled off through a door into what Marlene assumed must be a bedroom.

A moment later, the trailer's front door flew open and Sam Meyers and his surfboard filled a good part of the living area. He wore stylishly long shorts in a dark print and no shirt. Great abs, though a tad on the skinny side for Marlene's taste. Sam was tall, dark, and too geeky to be handsome, but still an attractive man, not a boy like the rest of the boardsmen. Would she ever sleep with a man that young again? Hell, would she ever sleep with any man again?

"Hi." He smiled, revealing straight teeth. "What's going down?" He lovingly lowered the surfboard to the space behind the wall and the couch. Its ends stuck out on both sides. "I don't want this baby injured in the scuffle. The cops might get tough." Sam flashed another smile. "You must be one of Annette's allies from NOW, right?"

So he called his granny by her first name. How progressive. Now how much of the truth should Marlene reveal? Lying was much easier when mired in a few facts.

"Right on," Marlene said, sounding like a hippie cheerleader. Rah, rah, sis boom bah. Go, women! "I'm Marlene Friedman."

"Have we met before?" Sam stared at her.

He'd fed her an opening line. "Call me Marlene. You look familiar too. I've seen you on the beach, haven't I? Palmetto Beach, that is. I live there."

Sam laughed. "I live there too. Or maybe it just feels like

that while I'm waiting to catch a wave." If he'd heard about his fellow boardsman's death, he showed no emotion. And how could he not have heard?

"Sammy, you bad boy, did you smoke all my pot? I even searched under the mattress." Annette had emerged from behind the bedroom door.

"No, no, Annette, you hid it under the cover of the air-conditioning unit in the kitchen." Sam Meyers stroked his grandmother's arm, his long fingers lingering on the inside of her elbow, then swooped down and kissed her on the lips.

It took a lot to shock Marlene, but she gasped, involuntarily for sure, yet loud enough to catch Sam's attention. He stopped kissing granny and grinned at Marlene. "Didn't Beth tell you about Annette and me? All those other hot old broads in NOW think we're a cool couple."

For possibly the first time in her life, Marlene was speechless.

"Our trailer park has as many rules as any fancy condo, you know." Sam sounded earnest, seeming to want Marlene to understand. "Only the owners' kin can visit for more than a week. Lovers don't qualify as kin. So for the record I'm Annette's grandson." Sam winked. "But we're saving up to get married. Then we'll be husband and wife and can live here legally. We don't like to break the rules, but true love conquers all, right?" He squeezed Annette's shoulder. "I can't believe no one told you about us. Annette and I are going to be featured in the chapter's newsletter."

Marlene shrugged, trying to present a calm exterior while her mind whirled. "I just joined the Fort Lauderdale chapter, haven't even gotten my membership card yet." She could feel sweat forming in her armpits and across her back, her silk jacket clinging to her body.

"The locals are late," Annette said. "Beth must have screwed up." She slid out of Sam's arms and walked around the long, narrow counter separating the tiny kitchen from the living/dining area. "You ready for another beer, Marlene?"

If she didn't need another drink now, when would she? "Yes, thanks."

"I'm smoking, with a beer chaser." Annette lifted a plastic bag out from under the cover of an ancient air conditioner in the kitchen window. "The pigs may rough us up and the pot helps my arthritis."

Marlene felt as if she had landed in a really bad movie circa 1969, where the hippie heroine had been transformed into an old lady.

Sam rolled the joints while Annette served the beers. Such a sweet domestic scene. Hell, somewhere the sun had to be over the yardarm. Marlene grabbed the can of Miller and drank with gusto. Maybe, while waiting for the protest to start, she could ask a few questions, like where did this odd couple meet and how Sam had hooked up with the surfers. He didn't appear to be grieving Jon Michael's death.

A very precise roller, not dropping a bit of weed, Sam worked on his second reefer. Annette had lighted hers and the sweet smell of marijuana filled the trailer. Marlene wondered if she could just say no. "I fell in love with Annette the first time I laid eyes on her," Sam said, albeit unwittingly, feeding Marlene the right line once again.

"So, where did you two meet?" Marlene shook her head as Sam offered her a joint. She'd fretted for naught; he just stopped rolling and started smoking, seeming not to care that she wasn't joining him. "Here in Florida?"

Sam patted Annette's behind. "No. We met in Acapulco." Marlene almost fell off the bar stool she'd just straddled.

"Recently?" She almost choked on the word.

"Just last summer, though we were old souls together in several past lives, so we know each other real well," Sam said.

Humph. They'd probably shared company in previous incarnations with Mandrake the talking skull.

"You don't know what you're missing, Marlene." Annette inhaled. "This is good stuff. Imported."

"From Acapulco?" Marlene asked, thinking about the missing Amanda Rowling and the pain etched on her mother's face.

"No," Sam said, "way closer than that."

A loud crash rocked the trailer, followed by screaming and another ear-piercing blast. The old man Marlene had seen earlier came dashing through the front door. "They started early, Annette, drove a goddamn bulldozer right through the clubhouse, demolished it."

"Rally the troops, we've been attacked by fascists," Annette shouted over her shoulder as she ran out the door. "Come on, Sam! Move it Marlene! This is war!"

Nineteen

When the bridge went up for the second time since they'd pulled in line, and they were still on Neptune Boulevard behind a flatbed truck filled with rowdy teenagers, Kate knew they'd be late. She also knew Nick Carbone was not a patient man.

After eighteen months in Palmetto Beach, Kate found the view of the Intracoastal Waterway awesome. The wide expanse of blue water, its shores lined with mansions and palm trees on the mainland, restaurants and a marina on the island, and a sleek sailboat gliding by under the open bridge would have given her great pleasure if she weren't so antsy. But today, even the smell of freshly baked bread wafting over the water from Dinah's Restaurant didn't improve her mood. Sometimes the only way to deal with worry was to worry. And sometimes the best way to deal with worry was to act. She opted for the latter.

"Katharine, I want you to tell me where you were and

what you were doing all day yesterday. Even more importantly, I need to know why you and Jon Michael were fighting just before he went surfing on Sunday night."

When Katharine squirmed in the front passenger seat of Kate's new but secondhand white Beetle convertible and glared at her grandmother, Kate added, "If you don't tell me, I assure you, you'll have to tell Nick Carbone."

In the backseat, Jennifer groaned.

Kate, deciding there was no time for tact, said, "You'll get your turn, Jennifer."

The bridge started to ease back down. Kate stepped on the gas pedal. "We'll be at the police station in less than fifteen minutes. Start talking, Katharine."

"I already told you, Nana. I wanted to kill Jon Michael."

"Oh God, don't say that," Jennifer shouted.

Jennifer had dressed in ten minutes flat and still hadn't bothered to put on any makeup, convincing Kate that her daughter-in-law was frantic. What did Jennifer know that Kate didn't?

"Let Katharine talk." Kate's tone sounded kinder.

"There's another girl. I overheard him and Roberto quarreling about her earlier Sunday evening on the pier. I couldn't ask Jon Michael about her while Roberto was around, so Sunday night I snuck out of the apartment around eleven thirty and went down on the beach and waited for him."

"Didn't Roberto always surf with Jon Michael late at night?" Kate asked.

"Yes, but I'd heard Roberto say he wouldn't be going on the run Sunday night, and I needed to talk to Jon Michael."

"On the run." Kate found that an odd way for Roberto to describe whatever the boys did on those midnight rides.

"Katharine, why did you throw yourself at that boy?" Jennifer asked in a teary voice.

"Quiet," Kate said, shocking herself. "You'll have your turn." She heard Katharine stifle a giggle. Great, by the tune she finished this inquisition neither her daughter-in-law nor her granddaughter would be speaking to her. But she couldn't stop now. "Go ahead, Katharine."

"What do you want to hear, Nana? I told you this before. He said he never loved me and I shouldn't have followed him here, and his last words were, 'Take a hike, bitch.'"

Kate looked at Jennifer in the rearview mirror. "Okay, your turn. Where were you Sunday night? And don't say you were with a client if you weren't. Nick Carbone will know you're lying."

"How can this be a homicide investigation?" Jennifer whined. "That boy was killed by a shark."

"Mom, tell Nana the truth. I know you weren't with a client."

A strangled moan escaped from Jennifer, but she said nothing.

Katharine spun around and faced her mother. "You were on the beach, Mom, hiding behind the lifeguard's station. I saw you there when I started back to the condo. Jon Michael was standing in the surf. What happened after I left?"

"Are you accusing me of murder?" Jennifer shrieked, and then broke into sobs. Uncontrollable sobs filling the car, overpowering in their anguish.

Whatever reaction Kate had expected when she started asking questions, it hadn't been this.

"No, Mom, just of spying. Please don't cry. I know you could never kill anyone." Katharine sounded on the verge of tears herself. "I'm sorry, Mom. I love you."

"I love you too," Jennifer said, still sobbing.

Kate smiled. If nothing else, her probing had brought her granddaughter and her daughter-in-law back together.

They would need a united front when facing Nick Carbone.

"Mom, I saw you leave the beach just as Jon Michael rode that big wave."

Good Lord, maybe mother and daughter could alibi each other after all.

Twenty

Splayed, her arms and legs akimbo, Marlene lay flat on her back between Annette and Sam on the grass in front of what was left of the Rainbow Beach trailer park's clubhouse.

The old man had exaggerated. Only the picture window wall facing the ocean was gone. The pool side and the clubhouse's front and back walls were still intact. Out of the corner of her eye, Marlene watched an elderly lady in the pool floating on her back. "I can't get down on the ground, so I'm protesting from here," she'd said.

The woman wore an old-fashioned white bathing cap complete with a chin strap and trimmed in flowers made of pink rubber. Marlene recalled her mother had worn one just like that, only with turquoise flowers that matched her swimsuit.

The mayor and the builder paced at the rear of the clubhouse as the press and television anchors peppered them with questions.

Several of the elderly protesters were singing "God Bless

America." The grumpy old man, whose name was Mike, along with three other old men, had dressed in their uniforms from World War II: one from the Navy, one from the Air Force, and two from the Army, including Mike, who had been awarded the Purple Heart. The Air Force guy couldn't zip up his bomber jacket. A good thing—the temperature at midday had to be over ninety. The former Navy officer was quite dashing in his summer dress whites.

Dozens of teenage volunteers, of varied ethnicity, all clean-cut and attractive, had been recruited by Annette from the local high school. Well trained, they were applying cold compresses to the protesters' faces and giving them sips of water from small plastic glasses. The kids kept shouting, "Shame, shame, save Rainbow Beach," as they went about their ministering. Jesse Jackson could take lessons from Annette Meyers.

The construction workers, stymied, sat near the bulldozers, except for two or three who were helping the teenagers serve the water.

The police stood around looking sheepish. None of them wanted to be the first to haul some old lady off to jail and have his picture, resembling a storm trooper, plastered on the front page of the *Palm Beach Gazette*.

On the other hand, if she lived through this, Marlene could look forward to seeing herself on all three networks, plus cable. Of course, she wasn't being photographed from her best angle.

"Hang in there, Marlene," Annette said. "I'm sweating so hard my hand may slip out of yours. We need to maintain a united front." Annette had raised her voice, beseeching the other owners not to give up. "Please hold tight and hang in there, everyone."

When the first ambulance, siren blaring, arrived five minutes later, the mayor caved.

The builder had left the premises. Heat exhaustion, someone said.

At an instantly arranged press conference, the mayor promised Annette Meyers and the trailer park board that he would call a special town council meeting and ask the council to vote to reverse the earlier legislation—all the council members were nodding like sycophants—and then he'd introduce a bill to protect the Rainbow Beach trailer park. Hell, he'd turn it into a landmark.

At the impromptu potluck victory party in the remnants of the clubhouse, miraculously the air-conditioning was still working—though with one wall missing, it wasn't very effective—Marlene found herself dancing with Sam Meyers.

Mike, the former Army private first class Purple Heart winner, had brought a phonograph, circa 1950, and all his old 78 rpm records.

The old lady who'd been floating in the pool had brought homemade potato salad, and Annette was slicing a honey-baked ham. The owners must have counted on a victory; they just kept arriving bearing all sorts of great food and drink. The attractive former Navy lieutenant was making margaritas.

"I'll be seeing you," Sam crooned as he led Marlene in a well-executed fox-trot. Had Annette been giving him lessons?

Her partner seemed a little high and more than a little flirtatious. Marlene decided now would be the time to lob her questions.

She remained undecided about whether to flirt back. Would it get her anywhere? Or did Sam just have a thing for all old broads? Maybe taking a direct approach would be better. After all, this guy had been in Acapulco. Sam Meyers could have been involved in Amanda Rowling's disappearance. And "Granny" could have been too.

"So, is it just a coincidence you and Annette have the same last name?" She asked as he led her out of a graceful dip. That sounded innocuous enough, didn't it?

"You still think we're related, don't you?" Sam spun her out, more like a lindy movement than a foxtrot.

So much for innocuous. "God no, of course I don't." She didn't, did she?

"My real name is Samuel Levin. I changed it when I decided to move in with Annette. Lots of people in South Florida change their names to hide their real identities; I changed mine to make Annette and me more convincing as grandmother and grandson. But I'm sure you've figured that out."

Sam Meyers née Levin might be many things, but dumb wasn't among them.

"I'll Be Seeing You" ended and the strains of "The White Cliffs of Dover" filled the room. If she weren't trying so hard to interrogate Sam, Marlene would really be enjoying herself. "Let's keep dancing," she said, hoping she didn't sound desperate.

He gave her a sly smile and pulled her closer.

Maybe she needed to toss some truth into the mix. "My best friend and I live in Ocean Vista. Her granddaughter is Katharine Kennedy. Do you know her?"

"Yeah, she's the redhead who followed Jon Michael to Palmetto Beach, right?"

"Had you met her in Acapulco?"

"She'd split before I got there. The only woman I met in Mexico was Annette."

"The other three boardsmen knew Amanda Rowling. Did you?"

"Like I said, I only met one woman in Acapulco." He loosened his hold on her. Maybe she'd better switch gears.

"Such a tragedy about Jon Michael, wasn't it? Such an awful way to die."

"Is there a good way, Marlene?"

She was getting nowhere fast. Yet she had a hunch that, despite his glib answers, Sam was an okay guy. He worked in the computer field, saving his money so he could get married, held a full-time job while protesting against greedy developers, seemed to love Annette, and maybe loved women in general. Marlene loved men in general, so who was she to judge?

Acting on her hunch, she said, "You seem more grounded than the other surfers, Sam. I hate to see our Katharine mixed up with that unsavory lot."

Sam's heel landed on her big toe. His first misstep. "Funny you should say that Marlene. Jon Michael was the best of the bunch and that's not saying much. That sociopath Claude Jensen should be in jail like his father the ax murderer. I'll bet there's more than one skeleton in that cracker's closet. And Roberto Romero's down there in Miami hustling his body and his soul for chump change. And some crazy old broad who wears her jewels to bed keeps him in threads."

"Why do you hang out with them?" Marlene's puzzlement was in her voice. And she'd check out that old broad who slept in her jewels.

"Make that past tense," Sam said. "I hung out with them, wanted to surf like them, learn how to catch a wave. The boardsmen were wicked, the coolest. Like in Acapulco, Jon

Michael and Roberto could have had any girl they wanted. Same here in Florida."

"But?"

"But I got fed up. It's time for me to put away my toys and settle down." Sam glanced across the room. "If you're done with your questions, I'd like to dance with my girl."

Marlene ate a hearty lunch—playing detective works up an appetite—drank two Diet Cokes, wanting to be awake for the drive home, and enjoyed a quick spin around the floor with the former Navy officer. He said he'd call.

All in all, not a bad day.

The last thing she saw as she drove out of the trailer park was the bumper sticker on Sam's truck: IF IT SWELLS, RIDE IT.

Twenty-One

Nick's office smelled of salami, just as it had the first time Kate's presence had been requested. She could only hope the aroma wasn't wafting from the same salami hero she'd spotted on his desk almost a year ago.

Everything else seemed the same: institutional green walls, cluttered desk, and no personal touches.

The detective looked the same too, though he'd lost a little weight: olive skin, Roman nose, and bushy brows, not the least bit handsome, yet perversely appealing.

Now as then, his type A personality filled the room, leaving none of the three women in doubt about who was running the show. Katharine almost, but not quite, cowered.

Kate, annoyed by so much attitude and the effect it had on her granddaughter, thought the detective could at least smile. Even the cops on *Law & Order* were courteous during a first interview. And she knew Charlie would never have behaved this way. She never should have dined with the enemy. Of course, she hadn't known Nick was the enemy then.

Katharine had visited Florita Flannigan Monday afternoon, but where else had she been? And why hadn't Jennifer contacted her daughter as soon as she'd arrived on Sunday? And where had Jennifer spent Monday afternoon? Had Jennifer and Katharine gotten together? If so, what had they talked about? Nick would ask them that. Kate felt sure that whatever Katharine and Jennifer, either together or alone, had done and wherever they'd gone wouldn't be incriminating, but she didn't like surprises.

"I'd like each of you ladies to tell me where you were on Sunday night when Jon Michael went surfing," Nick said, after a brief nod acknowledging their presence and a terse hello.

Humph, did the detective consider Kate a suspect too? Still, if he really suspected any of them, would he question all of them at the same time?

With mother and daughter providing alibis for each other and Kate having witnessed both Katharine on the beach and Jon Michael riding off on his surfboard—she'd felt no need to elaborate on their quarrel—Nick moved on. Kate knew it wasn't a pass, just a pause while he checked out the rest of their activities over the last couple of days.

"Alright, Mrs. Kennedy." Nick addressed Jennifer. "Please tell me when you arrived in South Florida and what you've been doing here."

"Wait a minute," Kate snapped. "Do we need a lawyer here? Why are you asking all these questions? How can Jon Michael's death be a homicide? How can my daughter-in-law and granddaughter be suspects in a shark attack?"

"A shark can be enticed to attack, Kate." Nick sounded less harsh. "And I'm just gathering information." The steely calm in his voice made Kate more anxious.

"How?" Katharine asked. Her voice quivered, but she met Nick's eyes.

"We found traces of pig's blood and a bit of wire on the sliver of surfboard the fishermen hauled in with the body and another trace of wire on the piece that washed up on the beach." Nick cupped his hands, moving them up and down like scales. "A shark warning had been posted. Pig's blood would attract a shark. As for the wire, both pieces were found on the underside of the board. Maybe part of a wire basket or cage, used to transport some sort of contraband protected in strong plastic." He shrugged. "Like marijuana. Might explain the midnight surfing."

"That's crazy," Katharine said. "Transported from where, Detective Carbone? They couldn't have surfed all the way to Bimini for a drug deal, could they?"

"That's exactly what Roberto Romero said before I pointed out that he and Jon Michael might have made the drug transfers from a boat." Nick smiled, a snide sort of smile. "Of course, Romero denied everything in two languages. The feds are talking to him now."

Kate—stunned and, worse, scared—reeled, glad she was seated. If Jon Michael had been murdered, then Jennifer and Katharine being at the beach together at midnight watching him go surfing didn't prove their innocence. One of them could have planted pig's blood in the cage much earlier. Indeed, one of them might have been there to make sure Jon Michael took off on the rigged board. Fear mixed with guilt made for a heavy heart and a sour stomach. Kate's fingers shook as she rummaged through her handbag for a Pepcid AC.

Nick turned from Katharine to Jennifer. "Now, Mrs. Kennedy, that brings us back to your activities since you arrived in South Florida on Sunday. For example, did you and Roberto Romero have a chat about Jon Michael being a threat to Katharine when you dined with him at the crepe place on Las Olas Boulevard yesterday afternoon?"

Twenty-Two

It hit her like the proverbial ton of bricks as she turned left on A1A heading south toward home.

When Annette had pulled the marijuana stash out from under the air conditioner cover, Marlene had seen something sparkle. There must have been a hell of a lot of sparkly stuff to shine so brightly and catch her attention. What with all those moral decisions she'd been making about whether or not to have a second beer and whether or not to smoke pot, she'd forgotten all about the glitter...and what it might be.

She swerved and made an illegal U-turn, just missing a yellow Rolls Royce heading north. The driver, in full chauffer livery, stopped short, rolled down his window, and made an obscene gesture. Marlene made an even more obscene gesture and almost knocked the scrolled RR hood ornament off the car as she sailed past the Rolls into the trailer park.

She thought she spotted the mayor peering out of the rear window. He didn't look happy.

The party was still in progress, though a few of the owners were heading back to their trailers. None of them paid any attention to her. She was just another old broad in a classic convertible, a common sight in Palm Beach County.

Marlene figured Annette would be holding court as Rainbow Beach trailer park's patron saint and savior for at least another half hour. And she knew the Meyers' door wasn't locked. Sam had left it open so they could replenish the beer in the clubhouse as needed. Even if she did get caught, she'd just say she'd forgotten her cigarettes. The Meyers would understand a craving that led to breaking and entering. Well, entering. Marlene believed it was less of a crime if the door was open. And hadn't she been a guest earlier in the day?

She parked several trailers away and strolled over to Annette's. Once in the living/dining area, she wasted no time. She ran around the counter and lifted the lid on the air conditioner. Sure enough, a dazzling array of jewels, neatly stacked in quart-size baggies, lay next to the plastic bags of marijuana. Clearly, Annette Meyers was another candidate for Diamond Lil. And, though the two women looked nothing alike, Annette's thick gray-streaked hair and Florita's thick white hair were not unlike the bank robber's. Annette's hair was longer and she was a larger woman than Florita, but both resembled the general, if somewhat garbled, descriptions of Diamond Lil.

Marlene heard a moan from behind the bedroom door. Jeez, she'd better get out of there. She dropped the air conditioner cover and then jumped as it banged shut. Pirouetting around the counter, she had her hand on the doorknob when Annette's voice stopped her cold.

She spun around, rehearsing what to say, but was

rendered speechless when she saw a half-naked Annette standing in front of the former Naval officer who wore purple silk boxer shorts and a sheepish grin.

"What are you doing here?" Annette shrieked.

"I forgot my cigarettes," Marlene managed to croak out.

Annette smiled. "That's all right, then. I was afraid Sam asked you to follow us. That boy is so provincial. I just hope his jealousy doesn't break us up. You have a safe trip home, Marlene." Annette turned and pushed her guest back into the bedroom.

Driving through Hillsboro Mile, with some of the priciest real estate per capita in the United States, Marlene firmed up her plans for the afternoon. First she'd pay a condolence call to Florita Flannigan, ask a few questions, and then she'd drop by Claude Jensen's house. Both Sam and Florita had painted him as a very bad egg. She wanted to see if the cracker lived up to his reputation. She'd felt sorry for Grace Rowling and, convinced that Claude and Roberto had been involved in Amanda's disappearance, Marlene had lots of questions for Claude.

She stopped at Dinah's for coffee. Funny how two beers in the morning had left her sleepy, even though she'd later washed them down with several Diet Cokes. Maybe she should have a slice of that fudge cake sitting under the glass on the counter. After all, they fed soldiers chocolate bars for energy, didn't they?

Why hadn't Kate called? Marlene pulled out her cell phone and shook her head. She'd forgotten to turn it on this morning and she had two messages from Kate. She glanced at her watch. Based on Kate's second message, Jennifer—and when the hell had she blown into town?—Katharine, and Kate might still be meeting with Nick Carbone.

As she drank her coffee, she asked Myrtle for a slice of cake, and then decided she'd drive by the Palmetto Beach Police headquarters to see if Kate's car was in the lot. She didn't want to call and interrupt the meeting. Kate had sounded frazzled. Jeez, did Nick Carbone think Katharine had been involved in Jon Michael's death?

Fortified with caffeine and sugar, two of nature's finest food groups, Marlene got in line to cross the Neptune Boulevard Bridge to the mainland.

The Palmetto Beach Police Department parking lot was jumping, with lots of squad cars coming and going. After New Year's Eve, Halloween was the busiest day of the year for the police. Kate's car was parked near a gleaming black Cadillac, bigger than Marlene's '57 convertible. Probably some pimp's car, she thought, and then started when Roberto Romero stepped out from behind an SUV the size of Chicago, opened the door to the Cadillac, and got in the driver's seat. It wasn't until Roberto was pulling out of the parking spot that she noticed the redhead in the front passenger seat: Mary Frances Costello. Marlene's second odd couple sighting in less than an hour and a half. Happy Halloween.

She drove on to her self-appointed rounds.

Florita Flannigan's house looked sad. A large black wreath covered a third of the Florida bungalow's front door, but that wasn't why. An aura of gloom had seemed to settle over the place, shrouding the house in sorrow. Marlene knew that, in theory, it wasn't possible for an inanimate object to have emotions, but she'd swear this house was in mourning.

The door opened and Florita greeted Marlene in tears. "My beautiful boy is dead."

"I'm so sorry." Marlene felt choked up and teary herself. Jon Michael's grandmother was suffering. Maybe Marlene shouldn't have come.

"Mandrake said you'd be stopping by." Florita grabbed Marlene's elbow. "Come in, I have a pot of coffee on. We need to talk about the pig's blood."

Twenty-Three

Jennifer had jumped out of her chair and verbally lashed out at Nick, making him very angry and her mother-in-law very nervous. A suspect, even an innocent suspect, shouldn't accuse the detective in charge of the murder investigation of being an intimidating boor.

"Sit down, Mrs. Kennedy." Carbone spoke softly. He must be furious. His tone frightened Kate.

Jennifer sat. He must have frightened her too.

Katharine twisted her handkerchief into knots. All color had drained from the girl's face and she was staring at her mother as if she'd never seen her before.

"Ladies, I have asked you all here together so you can tell me, and maybe each other, what you've been up to and why." Carbone sighed.

Jennifer flushed and turned away from Kate's scrutiny.

"Some of your collective and individual behavior has been baffling. Now, Mrs. Kennedy," the detective said, addressing Jennifer, "would you like to tell me your version of that luncheon conversation with Roberto Romero or shall I go with his, which indicated you'd found him hot and had used Jon Michael as an excuse to get to know him better?"

"That bastard," Jennifer stammered. Kate had never heard her daughter-in-law use that sort of language or sound so ruffled. "I wanted to talk to him about Acapulco. I believe Roberto, Jon Michael, and that other boy, Claude Jensen, had something to do with Amanda Rowling's disappearance. I knew those surfers were no good and Katharine was involved with them. I'd hired a private detective. They all had dicey pasts. For God's sake, Claude's been in jail and his father's an ax murderer. Roberto's a gigolo. I was worried about what might happen to my daughter." She faltered, seeming incapable of going on. The strain showed on her face.

Katharine hung her head, her face ashen, her eyes filled with tears, her shame almost palpable.

Jennifer Lowell Kennedy, stockbroker extraordinaire, society fund-raiser, perfect hostess, devoted wife and mother, looked haggard and helpless.

It made Kate mad. "Stop!" she shouted at Nick. "Enough."

The detective rolled his chair back and stood up. "This is a murder investigation, Kate. I'd think you of all people would want to hear the truth."

Why, because she was the widow of a homicide detective and she'd dabbled in detecting herself? How dare Nick use that rationale to tear her family asunder? Or could Nick be on the right track? Maybe she didn't want to know the truth.

"No, Kate. Let me finish," Jennifer said. "I want it all out, every lie, every evasion, and every motive. Then maybe Detective Carbone will look for the real killer and leave our family alone."

Nick sat back down. "I'm listening."

"I arrived in Fort Lauderdale late Sunday afternoon and checked into the Boca Raton Hotel. I had no client here. I met with the private detective I'd hired on Grace Rowling's recommendation. I knew Katharine had fallen for Jon Michael in Acapulco and was still obsessed with him. I wanted to learn all I could about the Four Boardsmen, so I'd called Grace, who was convinced Jon Michael had harmed her daughter—she couldn't accept that Amanda was probably dead—and that Claude and Roberto had lied to protect him."

Katharine groaned, lifting her head for a moment to give her mother a filthy look.

"The detective told me about Jon Michael's and Roberto's midnight surf rides. He'd suspected they might be running drugs, but he couldn't figure out how." Jennifer waved her right hand toward Nick. "Now we know."

Nick nodded, his face remaining noncommittal, but somehow seeming to acknowledge Jennifer's giving him credit.

"I went to the beach Sunday night to spy on Jon Michael and Roberto. Roberto turned out to be a no-show and, to my surprise, Katharine was there, quarreling with Jon Michael. Little did I know that my mother-in-law had a balcony seat for the entire scene." Jennifer smiled. A weak smile to be sure, but it lifted Kate's spirits.

"How could you, Mom?" Katharine was screaming. "You invaded my privacy and spied on me for months. God, you actually hired a private detective to follow me around. And you hid out down here, sneaking around, checking up on me. It's like one of those bad fifties movies that we all laugh at in film critique class."

"Please continue, Mrs. Kennedy. What did you do on

Monday before Jon Michael's body was discovered?" Nick said, ignoring Katharine's rant and giving Jennifer no chance to respond to it.

"I had dinner with Grace Rowling. She's staying at Pier Sixty-Six. She was very concerned about Katharine, thought the surfers might harm her too. And Grace had discovered Sam Meyers, aka Sam Levin, the fourth boardsman, had also been in Acapulco when Amanda disappeared, though the Mexican police have never questioned him and he never came forward."

"Grace Rowling came to see me Monday night after Marlene and I returned home from the pier, from seeing Jon Michael's body." Kate hadn't meant to interrupt; the words just tumbled out. "Grace told us Katharine might be in danger, and she needed to talk to her." Without planning to, Kate had confirmed at least part of her daughter-in-law's report about her conversation with Grace.

Jennifer sighed. "My heart breaks for Grace and I like her, but it's obvious the woman had a motive for killing Jon Michael."

Nick turned to Katharine. "Speaking of motives, Roberto has attributed one to you. On Sunday evening, around eight o'clock, were you at the Neptune Inn bar with Jon Michael, Roberto, and Claude?"

"Yes, I was there." Katharine held her head high now, but her voice sounded strained. "Jon Michael and I fought about money. I'd refused to lend him any more."

"And what else?" Nick prompted.

Kate steeled herself.

"He shouted at me," Katharine said, her words so low Kate had trouble hearing her. "He said he didn't need my money anyway, that he hated my red hair and freckles, that I reminded him of Huckleberry Finn, and that I should go back to New York City where I belonged."

"Then why did you follow him to the beach at midnight?" Nick asked.

Kate prayed, hoping Katharine wouldn't repeat what she'd told Kate this morning: "I wanted to kill him."

"For the same reason I visited his grandmother yesterday afternoon," Katharine replied. "For the same reason I'll go to his funeral. I loved him. He was no good, but I loved him. Can you understand that? You have been in love, haven't you, Detective Carbone?"

Nick's olive skin darkened and his eyes telegraphed an emotion Kate couldn't read.

The phone on his desk rang. Nick picked it up and balked, "Carbone."

Kate watched as his face crumbled into deep furrows. "Okay, thanks." Nick hung up. "The hotel chambermaid found Grace Rowling dead in her bathroom."

Twenty-Four

Marlene never had put much faith in parapsychology, though she had taken an extension course from Duke University over forty years ago during her first marriage. She'd had the lowest rank in ESP in the entire class. No hearing voices. No predictions that came true. No seeing dead people. However, she didn't doubt that some people had seen dead men walking...and talking. People like Mary Magdalene.

She did countenance the idea of reincarnation, hoping she'd come back with Kate and at least two of her three husbands. And she'd behave better the next time around.

Though she enjoyed tarot cards and astrology, and the occasional visit to a favorite fortune teller in the Keys, she'd never consulted a medium. Now, apparently, she'd become one.

Despite Florita's very real grief, it had soon become crystal clear that the owner of the only tanning salon/talking-head operation in South Florida not only believed in Mandrake's ability to communicate with the world beyond, she also believed she'd been receiving messages from there, specifically from her grandson Jon Michael. Mandrake had sensed Marlene might be a medium; however, though he regretted it, he couldn't attend the séance.

Before testing her otherworldly skills, Marlene was sitting through a dissertation about pig's blood, based on information garnered from a dead surfer. Marlene wished she could swallow it with something stronger than tea.

Had Florita lost her mind? How could pig's blood be connected to Jon Michael's death? Why wasn't Mandrake joining them? And when had Marlene become Florita's confidante? Based on her hostess's miserable attitude when Marlene had left here yesterday morning, that would have required a loaves-and-fishes-size miracle.

"Let's see if I've got this straight, Florita." Marlene used a soothing tone, very different from her usual pitch. "Jon Michael contacted you from the grave to discuss pig's blood."

"Of course not," Florita said, shaking her head. "Jon Michael isn't in the grave yet. His body is at the coroner's, but his soul is in the Light."

"I'm confused," Marlene said, thinking that admitting the weaknesses in her thought processing might further endear her to her hostess.

"Detective Carbone told me Jon Michael's shark attack might have been premeditated murder. They found traces of pig's blood on a piece of his surfboard and on a strand of wire too. They think his killer put the pig's blood in a plastic bag in a small wire cage that had been attached to the bottom of Jon Michael's surfboard, and then rigged it somehow so the blood would seep into the ocean and attract the sharks."

Marlene's head reeled, thinking what a diabolical way to murder someone, and what an awful way to die. "How was the cage rigged?"

"I don't know," Florita said, "and neither do the cops. That's what you're here for, Marlene." She shook her head, the thick white hair swinging from left to right. "Mandrake told me that when you rang the bell. You have to ask Jon Michael."

Hoping to stall that conversation, Marlene said, "Where would the killer have gotten pig's blood? It's not like it's on the shelf at the store."

They were sitting in Florita's kitchen, almost as clean as Kate's and very attractive and nostalgic. The blue gingham curtains on the windows and the Norman Rockwell prints in white frames on the walls reminded Marlene of Jackson Heights fifty years ago, before the world became weary and she became jaded. Marlene wondered how Florita had decorated the talking skull's room. And she wondered where she'd stashed the Rolex and her other expensive jewelry. Maybe because she was in mourning for her grandson, Florita wasn't wearing any.

"There are three or four religious sects in South Florida and a few witches' covens, not to mention the devil worshippers, who use animal blood in their rituals," Florita explained, as if talking to a child. "Several butchers in Broward County have thriving sidelines, packaging and selling chicken blood, lamb's blood, and pig's blood." Her voice broke. "My grandson's killer wouldn't have had any problem finding and purchasing the murder weapon." She moved the teacups off the table. "Let's get this séance started. Jon Michael's death must be avenged."

"I need to use the bathroom first, Florita. Where is it?"

"Go down the center hall; it's the second door on the right. I'll get the candles."

Marlene figured she had three minutes to find Mandrake

and, maybe, the jewels. She was convinced if she found one, she'd find the other. And the bungalow wasn't very big.

She took the first door to the right and walked into total darkness. Bingo. This had to be the skull's digs. She fumbled along the wall for a light switch and found it, after working her way around three walls, feeling totally disoriented. Mandrake sat on a pedestal atop an oak table covered in a fine white linen cloth in the middle of the room. Marlene peered at him. The crystal skull, complete with deep eye sockets and crooked teeth, some of them missing, appeared heavier than twenty pounds and less ghoulish than Marlene had expected.

Except for a large armoire, there was no other furniture. The windows—Marlene had no clue which direction they faced—were draped in maroon velvet. The crystal chandelier rivaled the Phantom of the Opera's.

Could the jewels be in the armoire? She ran across the room, yanked the cabinet open, and stared at a display of recording equipment, a veritable miniature studio, capable of producing sound effects on cue.

Marlene sensed rather than heard the door creak. Panicked, she darted back across the room, thinking she could hide behind the drapes, but in her haste she fell against the altar-like table. The skull crashed to the floor as his owner screamed, "You stupid cow!"

Twenty-Five

"Do you think Grace was murdered?" Jennifer asked as soon as they drove away from the police station. "She'd skipped dessert at dinner last night because I said I was watching my figure. Damn, I wish Grace had ordered that blueberry torte with vanilla ice cream." Jennifer, sounding wistful, sighed. "I wish I had too."

Kate did, indeed, think Grace Rowling had been murdered, but she said nothing. A weary Nick Carbone seemed to have come to the conclusion that either Katharine or Jennifer might have killed Jon Michael. Both women had motive and opportunity, though the means—getting and placing pig's blood in the wire cage—were murkier. Since Kate felt certain that the two deaths were connected, she'd have to sort this out, find the real killer, and clear her granddaughter and daughter-in-law.

She'd begin now. "When Grace Rowling visited me last night, she neglected to tell me she'd had dinner with you, and

I presume that was at your request, Jennifer. But Grace did say she needed to talk to Katharine." She turned to her granddaughter, sitting next to her in the front seat. "Did Grace get in touch with you after she'd left Ocean Vista?"

"No," Katharine said, staring out the passenger-side window.

Kate heard evasion in the girl's voice and she'd had quite enough of that. "So you've never had a conversation with Grace Rowling?"

Katharine squirmed, trying to inch as far away from her grandmother as possible in the small convertible.

Outside the day looked like a chamber of commerce ad: the Intracoastal Waterway sparkled as they crossed the bridge and soft white clouds dotted the pale blue sky. The top was down, the sun warmed their cheeks, and a hint of color had returned to Katharine's face.

"Answer your grandmother," Jennifer said, tapping her daughter's shoulder.

Kate whipped around and glared at her daughter-in-law, who shrugged, but shut up.

"So what if I did?" Katharine kept her eyes focused on the boats in the water below them.

"No more secrets, Katharine. Nick Carbone will be asking you a lot more questions and you can't lie or even evade. Now tell me the truth."

Kate had come across harsher than she'd intended, but she'd remembered Katharine saying, "I wanted to kill him, Nana," and fear motivated her, coloring her judgment.

"Okay, I'll tell you."

Maybe fear wasn't such a bad motivator after all.

"By the time I got Grace Rowling's message last night, I was already with Mom up in the Boca Hotel. She was packing to move down here and I'd just heard from Claude that Jon Michael was dead, so I didn't call Grace back. I tried her hotel room early this morning, but there was no answer." Katharine gulped. "Maybe she was already dead."

"There's something else, isn't there?"

Kate didn't doubt that Katharine had told the truth...just not the whole truth.

"Yeah," Katharine said as Kate turned onto A1A heading home.

To Kate's amazement, Jennifer didn't comment.

"I met Grace Rowling on Monday morning before I went to visit Florita Flannigan and her talking skull."

So Kate now knew where her granddaughter had been yesterday, but she had no idea what had transpired. However, she'd zeroed in on the fact that Claude had called to tell Katharine about Jon Michael's death. And, at the moment, Claude Jensen was Kate's prime suspect.

"I hadn't seen Jon Michael since he took off on that wave Sunday night, but I couldn't stop thinking about him," Katharine said.

Jennifer stirred in the backseat; Kate swung around, giving her a look that could kill. Jennifer sat still, saying nothing.

"Grace and I met at Pier Sixty-Six; it's very pretty there, surrounded by all that water and those beautiful yachts. We had brunch on the patio. She told me the boardsmen were criminals, that she had evidence that could put Jon Michael, Claude, and Roberto in jail." Katharine turned to face her mother. "Did she tell you that too, Mom?"

Jennifer hesitated, maybe waiting for Kate's okay, then spoke. "Not in that detail, darling. Still, Grace's story frightened me enough that I called you right away, then checked out of the hotel and moved to Nana's to be at your side. I'd believed Grace when she'd said the boardsmen were dangerous; she never mentioned evidence, but I'd bet it was about the drug smuggling."

"One of them must have killed Grace," Katharine said, catching her breath.

Kate pulled into Ocean Vista's parking lot. "That doesn't explain who killed Jon Michael." Or why neither Katharine nor Jennifer had revealed these details to Nick Carbone. To be fair, the news of Grace's death—and they hadn't been told she'd been murdered—had stopped Nick's interrogation midstream.

Still, Kate wondered if her daughter-in-law or her granddaughter would have told him everything. Did anyone ever tell all? People forget. Or deny, even to themselves. Or color their memories to their advantage. And sometimes details or nuances honestly escape them.

The Ocean Vista lobby festered with holiday spirit. Sunday's pre-Halloween celebration on the beach hadn't sated the purists. This was October 31 and by God they were going to celebrate.

Unadorned, the lobby, decorated with a hodgepodge of statues of Greek and Roman gods frolicking in a huge fountain and more marble than Michelangelo had used to carve David, overwhelmed visitors. Most of the residents had learned to live with its gaudy ostentation.

Today bad taste had risen to new heights. Literally. Hundreds of orange and black balloons, along with witches, warlocks, ghouls, goblins, and ghosts hung from the rafters. Orange and black streamers were wound around the statues of Aphrodite and all those cupids in the fountain pool, and jack-o'-lanterns glowed on every table.

About a dozen condo owners, all in costume, were drinking cider while filling their trick-or-treat bags. Would the old codgers really go knocking on doors in the neighboring condominiums?

Mary Frances Costello was dressed as Raggedy Ann, which was better than Barbie, Kate thought, and not inappropriate for a woman whose doll collection and dance costumes had taken over her apartment. Who was her Raggedy Andy? Behind that makeup lurked a young face and, even in his baggy costume, Kate could see that he was toned and buff.

"I'm going up to the apartment, Kate," Jennifer said, heading toward the elevator. "I need to call Lauren."

"The good sister," Katharine said. "The one with the Lowell genes."

Kate laughed, laughter accompanied by a pang of guilt. She'd often felt that way about Lauren herself. No question Katharine had been Charlie's favorite granddaughter, and Kate's too. She wondered how much her son Kevin, just promoted to battalion chief in the New York City Fire Department, had known about Katharine's love affair with the surfer and her mother's relentless efforts to squash it. Very little, she'd wager.

"Kate," Mary Frances called. "Over here."

Kate cleared a path and walked past Batman, the Phantom of the Opera, and the Cowardly Lion to the reception desk where Miss Mitford reigned supreme. Katharine trailed behind her.

"Hi, Mary Frances," Kate said, peering at Raggedy Andy.

"I feel as if I'm in a Monopoly game, Kate. And winning.

Look who I got out of jail." Mary Frances giggled, gesturing toward Raggedy Andy.

"Happy Halloween, Señora Kennedy." Roberto Romero smiled, baring those perfect teeth.

Twenty-Six

"So Mary Frances is sleeping with the enemy?" Marlene asked, reminding Kate of her own earlier thought about dating the enemy.

She'd heard just the slightest touch of envy in her former sister-in-law's voice and measured her response. "I don't think Mary Frances is sleeping with anyone. She's a virgin, remember?"

"It's not like being a Floridian, Kate. Or a New Yorker. You don't have to pack. Virginity is a state you can move out of by simply dropping your drawers or your morals. I think our former nun was ready to rock and roll and Roberto was there to dance with her." Marlene's tone brooked no argument.

They were sitting at the pool, savoring the soft rays of the late-afternoon sun and catching each other up on their adventures. Katharine, perhaps sensing that the two old girlfriends needed some time alone, had taken Ballou for a long walk. Kate had figured Katharine needed some time alone too.

Jennifer, saying she had to do some work, had retired to Kate's guest room, where no doubt she was on her cell phone buying and selling oil futures in Istanbul or Timbuktu.

They'd all agreed to have dinner at Dinah's at seven. The restaurant, a true early-bird establishment, closed at nine thirty.

Tomorrow was All Saints' Day and Kate wanted to go to church in the morning. She hoped Katharine would come with her.

"Mary Frances has had crushes before," Kate said. "And to my knowledge, she hasn't made a move, literally or metaphorically, to consummate them. What worries me is that she's in a tango contest and hanging out socially with a man who might be a drug smuggler and a murderer."

"She must know Roberto's a suspect. She picked him up at jail, didn't she? And in his car." Marlene slid off the chaise and into the pool. "Most men don't let women drive their cars unless they're getting something in return. Especially long black Cadillacs. I'll bet some Miami matron bought him that pimpmobile. You think Mary Frances knows he's a gigolo?"

Kate heard a rustling sound and looked up to see Joe Sajak, dressed as Robin Hood and not too bad in tights, standing in front of her. "Where's Mary Frances? She promised to go trick-or-treating with me."

"Am I her appointment secretary?" Kate asked, sounding as mean as she felt. "I think she's with her new friend, Raggedy Andy."

"When that part-time lifeguard, Claude, was posting the NO SWIMMING and SHARK ALERT signs this morning, he told me that Mary Frances's new friend sells himself to older women. Did you know that?" Joe wagged his right index finger at her.

Kate smiled. "Maybe Mary Frances was the highest bidder." She stood and walked to the edge of the pool, brushing past him. He was almost in her face. "Happy Halloween, Joe." Though she hadn't planned to get her hair wet, she jumped in, splattering his costume and wilting the feather in his cap.

Fifty years ago, Marlene had been on the Olympic swim team. Kate, who did a sidestroke version of the dog paddle, didn't even try to keep up with her former sister-in-law. She swam for a while, and then lay on her back, her face warmed by the sun, glad she'd applied SPF 40 sunblock.

In a few minutes Marlene, who'd been doing laps, joined her.

"You got rid of Joe, I see."

They both laughed. She and Marlene often didn't need words. They seemed to read each other's minds, sense when one was hurting, feel the same response to people and their problems.

"Tell me about the skull," Kate said. "Will he live?"

Marlene shook her head. "I sure hope so." Her blonde hair had come out of its twist and was plastered to her scalp. Kate figured she'd be wearing a turban tonight. "You know I'm not into the occult."

They both laughed again.

"Okay, so I'm a little superstitious." Marlene pushed a strand of hair off her nose. "But I hope I didn't do any real damage. I ran out of there so fast, I'm not sure. And Florita's going to be mad as hell if she knows I found her sound effects."

"Was there a rug?"

"Nope, a marble floor."

Kate groaned.

"But there were Turkish carpets all over the place. I'm sure there was one in front of the skull's shrine."

Kate hoped Marlene was right.

"Poor Grace Rowling. I liked her." Marlene climbed out of the pool. "You think she was murdered, right?"

Kate watched her step. She wasn't nearly as agile as her much heavier sister-in-law. "That would be my guess," she said, as Marlene gave her a hand and helped her over the edge.

When Kate came into her apartment, a towel wrapped around her head and bundled in her white ankle-length terry cloth robe, she was surprised to see Jennifer dressed in a smart black pantsuit, her suitcase and computer bag at her feet.

"I'm flying back tonight, Kate. Thank God, Delta had a cancellation in first class. I have to see a client in Bangkok."

"What about Katharine?"

Her granddaughter stuck her head out of the kitchen. "I'm not going anywhere, Nana. Remember I promised Florita Flannigan I'd be at Jon Michael's funeral."

Kate wondered if her granddaughter would be willing to go home after the funeral, go back to NYU, pick up the pieces, and move on. This wasn't the time to ask those questions. Mother and daughter must have had a talk. Kate decided she wouldn't comment other than to say, "Katharine, you're welcome to stay, darling."

"Well, I'm out of here. I have to be at the airport so damn early and I have to return the rental car." Jennifer turned to

Katharine. "Take care of yourself. I'll see you in New York next week. Don't upset your father. Come home by Saturday."

Katharine kissed her mother's cheek, but, unlike with Florita Flannigan, she promised her mother nothing.

Not everyone celebrated Halloween. There wasn't a streamer or a jack-o'-lantern in sight, but Dinah's had a good crowd. Only Katharine was under sixty. Or so Kate thought.

A smiling Myrtle came over and greeted them. "Your granddaughter's so pretty, Kate; she must break all the boys' hearts." Kate wished she could give her favorite waitress a gentle kick in the shin.

Katharine just laughed and said, "Right" Kate felt proud of Katharine, knowing how hurt she was.

"Remember how we were talking about Granny Meyers the other day?" Myrtle asked, pointing to the door. "She and her grandson just came in. And it's not even Fish-fry Friday." Myrtle waved toward the couple. "I'm telling you, I never saw a more loving grandson."

Marlene tried to hide behind her menu. A turban covered her hair and she had her back to the door. Still Kate wondered how this scene would play out.

Katharine started. "I know that woman, Nana."

"From where, darling?" Kate asked.

"Acapulco. She used to surf with Claude Jensen. She hung out with him all the time. I always thought they were an odd couple."

"Do you want to say hello to the Meyers?" Myrtle asked.

"No," Marlene barked. "We're ready to order. I've had my fill of odd couples for today."

Twenty-Seven

Grace Rowling's death was the lead story on the eleven o'clock news. Kate seldom went to bed without her news fix. Her interest—what Charlie had called her *passion*—for current events was not a recently acquired taste, or a time filler, as it seemed to be for so many retired people, who'd turned watching the news into a "job."

Kate had thrived on newspapers and newscasts ever since she'd discovered Dorothy Kilgallen's column in the *Journal-American* and Edward R. Murrow's *See It Now* program on CBS television.

Since the Kennedy win at the 1960 Democratic Convention, her network of choice had been NBC. She'd gotten hooked on Huntley and Brinkley, and Kate was not a channel hopper.

So, though wiped out, she'd propped up her pillows and turned on the television.

The blonde anchorwoman was reporting from Pier Sixty-Six.

"Grace Rowling, mother of missing teenager Amanda Rowling who'd disappeared in Acapulco last August, was found dead in the bathroom of her Pier Sixty-Six hotel room this morning. In an exclusive to NBC News, the maid who discovered the body, Maria Lopez, tells us Mrs. Rowling was lying in the bathtub covered in blood, but she didn't see a weapon in the bathroom."

A picture of Grace and Amanda, two pretty women, smiling in happier times flashed on the screen. Sadness and empathy, reinforcing how unfair life could be, swept through Kate. Her eyes filled with tears.

The anchorwoman continued. "Though the cause of death has not been given, both the Fort Lauderdale and Palmetto Beach Police Departments are investigating Mrs. Rowling's death as a homicide, which may be connected to the death of a surfer, Jon Michael Tyler. The surfer is one of three young men who have been under an umbrella of suspicion in the disappearance of Mrs. Rowling's daughter, Amanda. Tyler was the victim of a shark attack that, according to police sources, is also being investigated as a possible homicide. Tyler's body was fished out of the Atlantic near the Neptune Boulevard Pier on Monday evening. Detective Nick Carbone of Palmetto Beach's homicide department had no comment."

Kate turned off the television and, too wound up to sleep, grabbed the yellow pad and pen that she kept on her nightstand and started plotting her next moves.

Jon Michael had been murdered on Sunday night, less than two days before his twenty-first birthday. Did that have any significance? Had someone, maybe some twisted soul, not wanted Jon Michael to reach legal age?

Tomorrow morning, after church and a spot of tea, she'd

fob Katharine off on Marlene and pay a solo visit to Claude Jensen.

Charlie always said watch out for the amoral. Sociopaths come in all sizes, all ages, all races, and both genders. They're often charming like Ted Bundy or brilliant like Hannibal Lecter, or seemingly innocent like the well-mannered little girl with blonde pigtails who'd killed her smarter classmate and the suspicious handyman in *The Bad Seed*. On Broadway, the "perfect" child had survived, undetected, to kill again. They'd softened the ending for the movie version.

When she'd filled a page on her yellow pad, she turned off the light and closed her eyes. The pillowcase smelled like Bounce, proving "unscented fabric softener" was an oxymoron.

Her heart felt as if it might leap out of her skin, and visions of ax murderers danced through her head. At twelve thirty she gave up, turned the light back on, and started on the next page.

So many questions on her list, but as Kate edited what she'd written she grew calmer. Unanswered questions, like unanswered prayers, offered an opportunity to learn. And Kate had a lot to learn.

The questions in random order on the first page addressed most of her concerns:

Why was Jon Michael killed?

What would the murderer have gained by his death?

Who knew about the wire basket under the surfboard? (That should narrow the field of suspects: Claude, Roberto, Sam, and, possibly, Annette Meyers and Florita Flannigan.)

Where had the pig's blood been purchased? (She'd try an internet search for Broward County butchers and see how many of them sold pig's blood.)

How were Jon Michael's and Grace Rowling's deaths connected?

Had Grace discovered who'd killed the surfer? (It would seem so, but Kate needed proof.)

Were the motives for the murders connected to Amanda Rowling's disappearance in Acapulco? (Kate had a strong hunch they were and she planned to talk to Claude, Roberto, and Sam.)

Where had each of them been at the time of Grace Rowling's murder? (Grace had been very much alive when she'd left Kate's late Monday night. The maid had found her dead in the hotel bathroom on Tuesday around noon. Who had visited Grace at Pier Sixty-Six during that time frame? No doubt, the police would check out the Boardsmen's alibis. However, the police wouldn't necessarily suspect Sam's "granny," Annette Meyers, who'd been surprisingly gracious when Marlene had introduced Sam and her to Kate and Katharine as they'd been leaving Dinah's.)

Kate's second page was shorter and even more random, with quirkier questions:

Why was Roberto romancing Mary Frances?

Who was the older woman in Miami who, according to Sam Meyers, wore her jewelry to bed and was supporting Roberto?

Could Florita or Annette or, maybe, Roberto's patroness be the infamous bank robber, Diamond Lil? And, if so, had the robberies somehow been connected to the murders? (Kate believed they were, but had absolutely no proof to back up that belief.)

She couldn't bring herself to put her final question on paper. Had Katharine or Jennifer been involved in either of the murders?

Twenty-Eight

Wednesday morning, November 1

St. John's in Lauderdale-by-the-Sea, constructed of brick and mortar and complete with a courtyard and a school, reminded Kate of a real church, a northern church. More than she could say about those pastel-colored, modern-when-built-in-the-seventies-but-now-showing-their-age, prayer-with-an-ocean-view churches dotting the South Florida coastline along A1A.

She sat at nine o'clock mass, contemplating the dead. She'd filled in the names of those she wanted remembered on her All Souls' Day envelope and then, having more souls to request prayers for than the ten spaces provided, she started on a second envelope. It was telling that she'd reached an age where she felt closer to more dead people than to live ones.

Though All Souls' Day was celebrated—maybe observed was a better word—on November 2, All Saints' Day, November 1, was the last day to fill in the spaces on the envelopes. Kate had followed this ritual for decades. She wondered if anyone would request prayers for her.

Katharine was off lighting a candle for her grandfather, whose name topped Kate's list. Maybe Katharine would become keeper of the flame for her grandmother too.

The priest was giving an uplifting if rather long homily. South Florida clergy seemed to believe their older parishioners had nothing to do. Kate had plenty to do this holy day morning, including finding a way to dump Katharine with Marlene while she tracked down a killer. She stopped listening to Father Dunne and started planning. But by the time she gave the sign of peace to her pew mates and to those in front of and behind her, Kate still didn't have a strategy.

Einstein Bros. Bagels, located in a strip mall on Federal Highway in Palmetto Beach, made bagels that almost tasted as if they'd been baked in New York. Not quite, but almost. Marlene would be meeting them there.

Jeff Stein, the young editor of the *Palmetto Beach Gazette,* waved to Kate and she introduced him to Katharine, thinking it was too bad he was married. Kate had written a few obituaries and an occasional feature story for Jeff over the last few months, and he'd been trying to hire her part-time. He joined them, reminding Kate that the offer was open. "Not much money, but you'll get a byline."

As Kate bit into her cinnamon raisin bagel, Marlene, almost on time, walked into Einstein's, and the strategy that had eluded her in church now flashed through her mind, clean and clear. "Hey, Marlene, grab a bagel. I have an assignment for you and Katharine."

Without much persuasion, Katharine and Marlene agreed to go with Jeff to the *Gazette* office and research the butcher shops that sold pig's blood. Jeff, maybe smelling an exclusive, said he'd be delighted to have them there.

"But Nana, I didn't get to see Florita Flannigan yesterday. I'd like to drop by there this afternoon."

Katharine knew nothing about Marlene's disastrous visit to Florita's yesterday, and Kate wasn't about to discuss it now.

"Fine. You and I will visit Florita this afternoon, but this morning we need to divide and conquer." Kate sounded like a drill sergeant. "I'm off to talk to Claude Jensen. After you and Marlene finish your research at the *Gazette,* please go talk to Mary Frances; find out what she knows about Roberto."

"What do you need to know about him?" Katharine asked.

Kate sighed. It was obvious Katharine hadn't inherited either Charlie's or Kate's gift of natural nosiness. "Everything. Start with where he lives. Or why Mary Frances picked him up at the police station. Find out if Mary Frances knows when and how he arrived here from Cuba. Oh, and see what you can find out about his lady friend in Miami. Aunt Marlene will know what to ask." Neither Marlene nor Katharine looked happy about spending the morning together. What had caused the strain between them? Kate decided she just didn't have time to worry about that now. "I'll meet you back at Ocean Vista at one." She almost shooed them off.

Kate, who'd gotten the address from the Palmetto Beach phone book under a listing for Claude Jensen, Jr., drove due west and then turned right into a run-down rental complex with a sign reading SHADY SHORES. Since the development had no trees, only scrubby bushes, and was more than ten miles from the beach, its name was a major misnomer.

Remnants of a broken gate led to three two-story apartment buildings with peeling gray paint and brown lawns. A boy walking his dog pointed to Claude's building at the northwest end of the property. Any farther west and he'd be living on I-95.

She climbed the outside stairs to a catwalk and looked for number 213. She wasn't surprised when the apartment turned out to be the last unit on the northwest. Claude's rear window must abut the highway.

The door opened to her first tap. A sleepy-looking Claude, wearing only dingy white cutoff shorts, blinked in the bright sunshine. "What do you want?"

"May I please come in?" Kate smiled, hoping she appeared grandmotherly and benign. "I need to talk to you."

"Why?" He scratched his chest. The "yes, ma'am" and other small courtesies he'd exhibited on the beach had vanished.

"I have a few questions about Jon Michael." She decided to go for the jugular. "It would be in your best interest to speak to me before the police question you."

"I already talked to the cops." He sneered at her.

"But you didn't tell them that you were on the beach Sunday night, did you?" She'd taken her best shot. If he hadn't been on the beach he'd slam the door in her face.

"Come in," he said. Kate was gratified to hear just a tinge of fear in his voice.

The small living room flowed into an eat-in kitchen area. Clutter filled the couch, the recliner, the kitchen table and chairs, and most of the floor. A narrow, relatively open pathway led to what Kate guessed was the bedroom. Its window would be the one abutting I-95. Based on the rest of the apartment, Kate figured the lack of a view didn't matter.

The junk would be too high for anyone to see out of the window anyway.

Ants paraded across a kitchen countertop, maneuvering around obstacles that would repel a less determined army. Unwashed dishes, greasy frying pans, and a sponge that probably hosted the bubonic plague were not impediments.

These ants had a mission and no mere man's debris could deter them.

A squeamish Kate steeled herself. She didn't know which she found more offensive: the apartment or the man who lived in it.

Thank God he hadn't asked her to sit down. They stood in the narrow aisle face-to-face like gunslingers in an old western.

"Who says I was on the beach?" His breath smelled like stale booze and he hadn't shaved; the blond stubble on his chin and cheeks was sparse, downy like a boy's in puberty. The elastic in his shorts was frayed. Kate hoped it held.

"I say so, Claude. I saw you there," she lied, meeting his eyes, but not knowing how to hide her shaky hands. She jammed them into the pockets of her khakis.

"That don't prove I did anything." The glaze left his pale eyes, maybe signaling that he had an idea. "Sure I was there; I was showing Jon Michael some moves. Sweet moves. And I was telling him how I might be getting a job teaching at a new surfing school down in Davie."

"My balcony has an excellent view of the beach, and I stay up late. I never saw you surf with Roberto and Jon Michael on any of their earlier midnight rides." Kate's right hand clenched in her pocket. When had the pig's blood been planted in the wire cage? It must have been shortly before Jon Michael had taken his last ride. One of three remaining boardsmen had to be guilty. Who else would have known about the wire cage under Jon Michael's surfboard? Or about a plastic bag that could be punctured to leak the blood? In the end, it always boiled down to motive, means, and opportunity. Kate felt besieged by mixed emotions: fear of Claude and joy that Katharine *probably* hadn't been aware of the cage. "Why did you lie to the police, Claude?"

"Are you stupid, bitch? I have a trial coming up for a DWI. I've served time. And my father's in jail for killing a girl." He started toward her. Kate screamed, spun around, and twisted the doorknob. She was still screaming as she hit the catwalk. An old man, two apartments away, opened his door just as Claude caught up with her, grabbing her shoulder.

"Morning, Claude. Nice day, ain't it?" The man winked at Kate. "I have my cell phone here." He opened his left hand to reveal a tiny phone, cradled in his palm. "It's programmed for 911."

Twenty-Nine

About halfway through their research at the *Gazette,* Marlene realized that she could have found these blood-selling butchers in the phone book. And how could they be sure that the killer hadn't just bought a pork loin at the supermarket and collected the blood drippings before roasting it? Kate, who obviously had more important work to do, hadn't wanted Katharine along. So she'd appointed Marlene as the designated babysitter.

    Jeff Stein had given them a private office and a computer, where Katharine had researched and then given Marlene the numbers to call. So far, one butcher had gone out of business, the second had already spoken to the police and demanded to know why Marlene was calling, and the third was being interviewed by Nick Carbone who'd taken the phone and asked Marlene what the hell she was up to.

    Royally ticked off, Marlene called a halt to their search. "We can get the rest of these numbers from information." She took off her headphone and placed it on the desk. "Enough, already. I say we go back to Ocean Vista and find Mary Frances."

Katharine laughed. "Nana has outfoxed us, hasn't she?" She stood and stretched. "Okay, let's thank Jeff and get out of here. Maybe we'll have better luck with the dancing nun."

On the way home, Marlene debated about confronting Katharine but decided to let it go. Maybe she didn't want to know which secret the girl knew; maybe it had nothing to do with Charlie. And Katharine might not know anything; Katharine might have outfoxed Marlene.

They arrived at the pool in time for the eleven thirty water aerobics dance class. Mary Frances stood in the shallow end of the pool leading six ladies and Joe Sajak in a wet version of the twist. Chubby Checker's voice boomed from a portable radio perched on the ledge.

Marlene jumped right in, causing quite a splash.

If she hadn't been burdened by her conscience—or lack thereof—and the babysitting job, Marlene the mermaid would have been really happy. She preferred water to land anytime. She even preferred sex in a waterbed. If she had to exercise, this was the only way to go.

"As we did last summer," the women sang along with Chubby, but Joe Sajak looked sullen, his mouth, for a change, clamped shut.

To think she'd chased after that jerk. But hell, what man hadn't she chased after?

"Breathe deeply," Mary Frances said. "Tighten those abs. Work those upper arms." She nodded at Marlene. "You're late. Double-time twists for you!"

Marlene could understand how some people would risk the gas chamber to remove irritants like Mary Frances from their lives.

Marlene held her head up, firming her neck muscles as she faced the sun. A bonus for working out in the pool was tanning as you tightened. The midday's rays were strong.

Mad dogs and Englishmen, Marlene chuckled to herself and turned her left cheek to the sun. They used to exercise at eight thirty, but Marlene had found that barbaric, often missing a session. Since Mary Frances's tango class now started at eight, she'd moved the water aerobics to eleven thirty. More civilized, but a hell of a lot hotter.

Did Roberto attend the eight o'clock tango class? Mary Frances had said he'd be her partner in this year's Broward County Tango Championship and most of the dancers, who'd competed year after year in that contest, had been the dancing nun's classmates. Roberto couldn't be getting much sleep, going surfing at midnight and then driving up from Miami for an eight o'clock class.

Maybe she'd spring for lunch in the post-hurricane, redecorated Ocean Vista dining room. Mary Frances might be more cooperative after a Scarlett O'Hara or two.

"Jumping jacks," Mary Frances yelled. She must have been hell on wheels in her nun's habit, bossing around all those convent school girls, and she hadn't lost her touch. She said jump and the old ladies asked how high. Gallons of water splashed over the sides of the pool as the class tried to please their teacher and surpass their personal best.

What annoyed Marlene most was that Mary Frances always looked so damn good. Even barking out orders, she glowed. Her naturally fair skin rosy, but not burned, her red curls swinging as she moved, and her green eyes seeming to twinkle in time to "Hard Day's Night" as she jumped higher than any of her students.

Joe Sajak left the pool before the Kegel exercises targeted

at women only began. Male anatomy didn't require strengthening the vagina muscles. Marlene wondered why she bothered. Would she ever have sex again? Well, one lived in hope, right? She listened up as Mary Frances gave an audiovisual demonstration.

Tiffani, who always drew a smiley face over the last *i* on her name tag and wore micro minis, waited on them. If possible, Tiffani was even perkier than Mary Frances. All this cutesy charm might make Marlene lose her appetite. Katharine's quiet negativity seemed like a social asset about now. Her grandniece—albeit by her second marriage to Charlie's twin brother, Kevin, but Marlene had always loved the child as if she were a blood relative—seemed to have turned sulking into an art form.

"I'm so sorry, Ms. Friedman. We've lost our liquor license." Tiffani delivered the line as if it were good news.

"How? Did it blow away in the hurricane?" Marlene needed a drink. And, though somewhat less urgently, she'd wanted to ply Mary Frances with Scarlett O'Haras.

Tiffani laughed. "No, ma'am, it expired. I know you served as condo president; maybe the new board isn't as efficient as you were."

"You got that right," Marlene said.

"I can offer you ladies wine or beer."

"Champagne?" Marlene sounded hopeful.

"Sure, I'll put a bottle on ice right now." The waitress turned toward the kitchen.

"Make it two, Tiffani," Marlene called after her as Katharine groaned.

They'd voted to stay in their bathing suits and dine

poolside at a table under an umbrella. Though she'd accepted Marlene's luncheon invitation, Mary Frances had explained that she had another engagement at three and she'd need time to shower and wash her hair before leaving Ocean Vista at two forty-five.

The former nun raised her flute. "To our hostess." She sipped the champagne with less enthusiasm than Marlene had hoped for.

Katharine didn't lift her glass. Not drinking? Or just not toasting her grandaunt?

"I'm so sorry about Jon Michael," Mary Frances said to Katharine. "I know he was a friend of yours and that you'd met in Acapulco."

Mary Frances had hit just the right tone, Marlene thought: sympathetic, but not cloying or nosy. She hoped she'd do as well when questioning Mary Frances.

"Did you talk to Jon Michael about me? You're one of Florita's clients, right?" Katharine sounded vulnerable.

Mary Frances reached over and patted Katharine's arm. "Yes, I am, but I didn't know Jon Michael was her grandson until she arrived at our pre-Halloween beach party with him." The former nun stared at her fingernails, and then removed her hand from Katharine's arm. "To tell you the truth, Katharine, at first I'd thought all the surfers were, well, disreputable."

"And meeting Jon Michael changed your mind?" Katharine asked, sounding dubious.

Mary Frances flushed, her sun-kissed skin blotched, then the glow returned. "No, meeting Roberto Romero changed my mind."

Marlene could almost hear Kate saying, "Wait, Marlene. Say nothing, just wait."

"Why?" Katharine asked. Exactly the question that Katharine's Auntie Marlene would have asked Mary Frances. Maybe there was something worthwhile about Kate's creative listening process.

"Roberto is so sensitive and so refined." Mary Frances shook her head, the red curls bouncing. "I don't know why he hangs around with those other young men, especially Claude Jensen. As I told Kate the other day, Claude is not only crude, but he has a family history of violence. Now I'm sure Claude's an evil man. A dangerous man."

Again, Marlene bit her tongue and drained her champagne flute, waiting for Katharine's response.

"And you know that Claude was in Acapulco when Amanda Rowling disappeared."

Well, that wasn't where Marlene would have gone, but Katharine might have opened up another box of unanswered questions.

Mary Frances nodded. "And I believe he was the blond who left the bar with Amanda that night."

Tiffani arrived, bearing three lobster salads. Though the presentation was divine, the waitress's timing sucked. Marlene felt like part of the scenery yet, for once in her life, she was more interested in listening than talking, or even eating. To make herself useful, she refilled all three flutes.

"Delicious," Mary Frances said, and then took another bite. "The new chef is a wonder, isn't he?"

Oh God, they were losing Mary Frances to the food; she was focusing on the lobster, not the boardsmen.

Katharine glanced over at Marlene. Did the girl need reinforcement? Was it Marlene's turn to pry?

"Roberto and I both think Claude murdered Jon Michael and that he probably murdered Amanda Rowling." Mary

Frances took yet another bite of salad. The woman was infuriating. "Do you want to know why?"

Joe Sajak, showered and changed, appeared out of nowhere. "May I join you lovely ladies?"

Marlene decided she'd have to kill him.

Thirty

"Where the hell is your daughter-in-law?" Nick barked in Kate's ear as she approached Federal Highway, heading for the Neptune Boulevard Bridge and then home. Damnation. She shouldn't have answered her phone.

Still shaky and needing comfort, Kate had wanted to tell Marlene and Katharine that Claude Jensen was a violent young man who indeed had been on the beach Sunday night. She'd driven straight from Claude's apartment to the *Gazette*. Jeff said Kate had missed them, that Marlene had seemed somewhat put off by her assignment and she and Katharine had left.

Kate may have missed Marlene and Katharine, but she couldn't escape from Nick Carbone.

"Jennifer's voicemail says she's out of the country."

Nick's fury fueled Kate's own. "You didn't tell her she couldn't leave, did you?"

"Well," Nick growled, "I didn't know then that Jennifer

had gone back to Pier Sixty-Six and saw Grace again later Monday."

Kate gasped, involuntarily to be sure, but there it was, out there for Nick to hear.

"And the medical examiner says Grace Rowling died from stab wounds inflicted between nine and midnight."

"Oh," Kate said. Jennifer had just become a prime suspect in two murders. If Grace had been stabbed between, say, nine to ten, Jennifer could have killed her before meeting Katharine later. And Jennifer had been on the beach on Sunday night too.

"I need your son's phone number at the firehouse," Nick said. "He may know where I can reach his wife."

Kate checked her cell phone's index and gave Nick Kevin's number.

"Thanks." Nick sounded a bit less angry.

"But you can't believe—" Kate was talking to a dead line. Nick had hung up.

Kate made an illegal U-turn on Federal Highway, generating several loud beeps and a few curses. She needed to talk to Florita Flannigan. She had to find proof that Claude Jensen had killed Jon Michael and Grace Rowling and that both murders were somehow connected to Amanda's disappearance in Acapulco. Claude and Jon Michael had been close for years. Florita had to know how cruel her grandson's friend was.

She'd explain to Katharine later, even go back with the girl to see Florita later today, but Kate had to do something right now to clear her daughter-in-law. She'd never realized how much she cared about Jennifer.

Kate stopped at St. Raphael's on Neptune Boulevard to get a mass card; this was, after all, a condolence call. Her next stop was a deli near the church where she bought sandwiches, fruit, and cookies. If she broke bread with Florita, she might get more cooperation.

As she pulled into Golden Glow's driveway, Kate left a message on Marlene's voicemail saying she was running late. For once she was glad Marlene hadn't answered her phone. She didn't even try to reach Katharine.

Florita opened the door on the first chime. Had she been watching out the window?

"I'm very sorry for your trouble," Kate said, as she'd heard dozens of her Irish American relatives use to commiserate in times of grief for more than sixty years.

She'd chosen just the right phrase for Florita Flannigan. "Come in, please. You're Katharine's grandmother, aren't you? Lovely girl, your Katharine."

"Yes, I'm Kate Kennedy. It's nice to see you again, though not under these sad circumstances." Another stock phrase at Irish wakes. She handed Florita the mass card. "Maybe we could go together."

By the time they sat down to lunch they were chatting like old friends. Kate might even get to meet Mandrake, unless, of course, Marlene had smashed the skull to smithereens.

"This must be so difficult for you, Florita. I can't imagine who would want to kill Jon Michael," Kate lied.

"Well, Mandrake and I have our suspicions."

Good. That must mean the talking skull was still in one piece. Kate nodded, giving Florita time to explain, to name the target of their suspicions.

"Do you know Marlene Friedman?"

Talk about out of left field. Where had that come from? Kate almost choked on her chicken salad.

"She's a very unstable woman."

"So I've heard," Kate said, hoping Florita would get back on track.

"Anyway, this mess all started in Acapulco." Florita took a bite of her sandwich and washed it down with tea. "My grandson has always been misunderstood, especially by women. Mandrake suspects one of the surfers. It could have been Sam Meyers, but I doubt that. He has the hots for Annette—that's his girlfriend—and I don't think he even knew Amanda Rowling, the girl who disappeared. Or it could have been that slime Roberto Romero, a gigolo, and, according to the Palmetto Beach police, a smuggler who'd led my grandson astray. All Four Boardsmen had been in Acapulco, but Claude Jensen was considered to be a 'person of interest' by the Mexican police."

And so was Florita's misunderstood grandson, Jon Michael, Kate thought, but remained quiet.

"That detective, Nick Carbone, told me they'd found shark's blood and pig's blood along with Jon Michael's blood on the bottom of his surfboard. The blood was on some cage that had probably been used to smuggle dope. Only a twisted mind like Claude's would have planted pig's blood."

"Twisted how?" Kate asked.

"Even as a kid, Claude killed small animals. I heard him tell that to Jon Michael. You know birds, mice, and once a neighbor's cat."

A classic sociopath, Kate thought.

"Amanda Rowling left the bar in Acapulco with a blond boy. It wasn't my Jon Michael; it was Claude."

"Do you have any proof of that?" Conjecture wasn't evidence.

"Do you believe me?" Florita asked.

Kate could hear the challenge in her voice.

Kate nodded. "I do, but we need some hard evidence about Amanda's disappearance or about her murder, if she's dead. And we need something that ties Claude directly to Jon Michael's murder." Something more than being on the beach on Sunday night. Hell, her granddaughter and daughter-in-law had been there too.

"Mandrake knows more. He had a rough time yesterday, but I'll let you talk to him, Kate. And I'll give you a big discount. Twenty-five bucks for fifteen minutes."

Thirty-One

"This is girl talk." Mary Frances waved Joe Sajak away. "I may let you into my aerobics class, but I won't let you into my mind."

Marlene was impressed. Maybe the dancing nun had turned into an ally. If Joe didn't move, Marlene would shove him into the pool, ruining all those neatly pressed clothes. He moved, disappointing her.

Katharine turned back to Mary Frances, "You were saying?"

"That I think Claude Jensen killed Jon Michael." Mary Frances paused, obviously enjoying Marlene's and Katharine's rapt attention. "Here's my theory. Jon Michael knew—and could prove—that Claude had killed Amanda Rowling. Claude killed Jon Michael to shut him up."

"And that theory would be based on?" Marlene couldn't keep quiet for another second.

"Stuff I've heard." Mary Frances sounded serious. "I'm wondering if I should talk to Nick Carbone."

"Try it out on us," Marlene said, trying to keep her voice neutral. She put her champagne flute down. She needed to concentrate.

"Okay, I'll try." Mary Frances sat up straight and glanced from Katharine to Marlene. "On Sunday, Roberto and I stopped by the Neptune Inn for a late lunch after rehearsing for the tango competition at the community center. Claude was at the bar, drinking shots; he was supposed to be working as the replacement lifeguard, but said he'd taken a break."

Marlene wondered if that happened before or after the shark alert had been posted.

"Claude was cursing out Grace Rowling, who'd followed the surfers to Palmetto Beach. He said, 'Yeah, I was in Acapulco, so what? The other boardsmen were there too. Jon Michael even offered to rub Amanda's surfboard with Sex Wax. We bought that blonde bimbo a couple of drinks, but she went to the head and never resurfaced.' Claude stared at Roberto and shouted, 'You was there too. You know goddamn well Jon Michael left with that girl. If she's dead, he's the one done it.' Then Claude turned to me." Mary Frances shook her head. "Among his other charming qualities, he's a bigot. He said, 'Those greasy Mexican cops questioned us for hours. Amanda's mother even hired a private eye and he followed me, followed all three of us. Nobody found nothing on me. That's cause there's nothing to find.'"

"But it sounds as if Claude was proclaiming his innocence," Marlene said. "What am I missing here?"

"What I didn't miss," Mary Frances said, sounding like her old, smug self. "You weren't a teacher, Marlene, or a high school principal, or a nun. I know when people are lying, trying to fob the blame off on a classmate, or playing 'poor me.'" She smiled, not unkindly, but more than a little patronizingly. "Believe me, Marlene; Claude Jensen was lying through those dreadful teeth."

Marlene smiled back. "What about Roberto? Your Latin lover was there the night Amanda vanished. That very same scenario, featuring Claude as the killer, could work for Roberto as well."

"It certainly could. Roberto is not above suspicion. Unlike Caesar, I don't require that in my relationships." Mary Frances sounded pragmatic, surprising the hell out of Marlene. Even Katharine started, and seemed about to say something, but instead sipped her champagne.

"Is that why you picked him up at the police station yesterday?" The dancing nun—doll collector, tango champion, and the world's oldest virgin—had surprised Marlene again. Mary Frances, a very annoying smart aleck, was also very intriguing.

"No, I drove Roberto there in his car. That Cadillac is harder to maneuver than some tango moves. Nick Carbone questioned Roberto for over an hour. Apparently," she smiled at Marlene, "the detective shares your perspective."

"What about you, Mary Frances? What's your perspective? Are you really convinced Claude's the killer? Or do you choose to believe that, so Roberto can be your dance partner and help you retain your Broward County Tango Champion title?" Marlene presented the former nun with what she hoped was a moral dilemma.

Mary Frances flushed again, redness creeping up from her neck to her cheeks. "Okay, Marlene, I don't think he murdered anyone, but let's discuss Roberto Romero."

All three women refilled their flutes. Marlene knew she could handle midday drinking, but she worried about Mary

Frances, who never drank much of anything, and Katharine, who wasn't even of legal age. This, however, was not the time for a temperance lecture. Marlene needed to focus on the murder case.

"I understand Roberto lives with a woman in Miami who sleeps in her jewels." Marlene relished the wide-eyed look on Mary Frances's face. "He told Sam Meyers the lady is his aunt and he also told Kate and me that he had an aunt in Miami. Have you ever met her?"

"No. He does talk about an aunt in Miami and he certainly never mentioned to me that she sleeps in her jewels, though I got the impression she has some money." Mary Frances frowned. "But Marlene, Roberto doesn't live in Miami. He lives right here in Palmetto Beach. I've driven him home after tango practice."

"Where?" Katharine asked.

"The Crest Motel." Mary Frances gestured south. "It's not far, one of those small places on the beach, heading toward Lauderdale-by-the-Sea."

As the breeze picked up and the powder blue sky darkened ever so slightly, Marlene made a mental note to drop by the Crest later that afternoon.

Mary Frances brushed stray hairs, blown by the wind, away from her cheek. "Why would Roberto tell Sam Meyers about his aunt—or whoever that woman is—sleeping in her jewels? Sam never seemed to be accepted by the other three boardsmen. I thought they only kept him around because he had a job and could pick up some bar tabs."

"Maybe they kept him around because he knew what had gone down in Acapulco," Katharine said. "That's what Grace Rowling thought."

Marlene wondered why Katharine hadn't mentioned that

before. So many crosscurrents in this case and so little ground gained.

Mary Frances stood and then staggered. "Dear Lord, I've had too much champagne. I feel a little queasy and I have to shower and dress for tango practice. What else do you want to know, Marlene?"

"Have you ever met Sam's girlfriend, Annette Meyers, the one he passes off as his granny?" Marlene stood too, pleased that she didn't stagger. "Annette has an impressive pile of jewels stashed under the cover of her air conditioner."

Katharine didn't stand. "Funny, Jon Michael's grandmother has a bunch of jewelry too."

Mary Frances nodded. "And Roberto is fascinated by that old lady, Diamond Lil, who's running around town robbing banks. He can't stop talking about her."

Thirty-Two

Kate had gone head-to-head with the skull and survived.

If she hadn't heard Marlene's saga about her brief encounter with Mandrake and how her former sister-in-law had discovered Florita Flannigan's recording equipment in the armoire, Kate *almost* might have believed the skull had something to say. Illusion can be heady stuff, but Kate had known it was all smoke and mirrors, or more accurately, great recording equipment and on-cue spooky lighting.

The skull, Florita's puppet, had only echoed his owner's sentiments.

Now driving over the Neptune Boulevard Bridge, the tantalizing smell escaping from Dinah's oven and filling the air tempted Kate to stop and buy a couple loaves of bread.

She gave in to temptation and further indulged herself with a black-and-white ice cream soda at the counter while Myrtle bagged the bread.

Kate noticed that her bottom had seemed to spread across the vinyl stool. Only another illusion, she hoped as she sipped her soda. She'd never had a weight problem, never even weighed herself, though her doctor did once a year. The number, up ten pounds from her wedding day, hadn't varied in years. Luck of the genes, she supposed; both her parents had been slim. And Maggie and Bill Naughton had loved ice cream sodas too. Still, feeling the spread, she considered buying a scale.

Myrtle pointed to the small television set behind the counter. "Hey, there was another bank robbery this morning."

Kate noticed the wide gold bracelet and two large-carat diamond rings as the waitress gestured with her right hand. Was every old lady in South Florida, except for Kate, a walking jewelry display case?

"Palmetto Beach is just a hotbed of crime, isn't it?" Myrtle asked, leaning in so close Kate could smell her perfume. Shalimar. The scent overpowered the aroma of baking bread. Kate, who wore no perfume, really couldn't stomach Shalimar. Marlene had gone through a phase in the fifties where each week she'd tried a different brand. Nina Ricci's L'Air du Temps had been the only one Kate could tolerate.

Kate nodded, backing away from the waitress.

"Murder by pig's blood, and is it five banks that Diamond Lil has hit?" Myrtle turned and peered at the television screen again.

A hidden camera tape of the bank robber filled the screen, revealing a rather blurry photo of an old lady in a white wig, topped by a tiara. Drop earrings reached her *Dynasty-era* shoulder pads, so wide they ended off camera. The royal blue, high-neck, long-sleeve dress appeared to be heavy brocade. Diamond Lil looked a bit like Queen

Elizabeth. Yet those eyes, hooded by deep wrinkles, reminded Kate of someone else. Who?

As Kate left Ocean Vista's parking lot, clutching her still-warm bread, she decided to check and see if Marlene or Katharine might be poolside before going up to her condo.

She found them sitting under an umbrella, the remains of their lunch, along with two empty bottles of champagne, still on the table. Mary Frances, wobbling a bit, was just leaving.

"Hi, Nana," Katharine said and then hiccupped. Had the girl been drinking? Kate, tired, cranky, and confused, glared at Marlene.

"I've been working on murder," Marlene said, as if that gave her license to kill.

"I'm out of here," Mary Frances said, "but there's one more thing I want to tell you about Roberto." Kate knew Mary Frances seldom drank, but she was tipsy today.

"Shoot." Marlene giggled.

Kate wanted to throw her sister-in-law in the pool—no, *drown* her in the pool.

"He and Claude have both been hired to teach down around Davie at that new surfing camp for women. I think it's called Women on Board. Under the circumstances, maybe they shouldn't be working there."

"You sure do save the best for last, Mary Frances," Marlene said, sounding considerably more sober. "Kate and I will check it out."

Kate shook her head.

"Don't act like Carry Nation, Kate; all that's missing is your ax," Marlene said. "I'll let you drive."

Kate heard snoring. She glanced over at her granddaughter. Katharine was sound asleep.

* * *

Forty minutes later, after three cups of coffee and a stern lecture for Marlene, Kate had walked Ballou and they were on their way down to Davie.

Katharine had made it upstairs and into her grandmother's guest bedroom where, with any luck, she'd sleep until they returned. Kate had explained that, though she'd already made a condolence call, she'd be happy to drive Katharine out to see Florita Flannigan tonight. Katharine, feeling awful, hadn't seemed to care much one way or the other. Kate figured Katharine had learned a lesson: lobster and too much champagne could be a lethal combination.

Driving south, Marlene apologized again, and then they caught up, each marveling at the other's exploits.

Davie had a flavor all its own. None of Fort Lauderdale's thriving-new-metropolis attitude, none of Hollywood's funky charm, none of Lauderdale-by-the-Sea's pretty, quiet quaintness. Davie was more like small town USA, only on the beach. On Federal Highway, pawnshops vied with gas stations and seedy bars. But the wood plank pavilion on the beach harkened back to days gone by, to an era when South Florida had offered escape and even solitude.

Kate found a parking spot a few blocks from the beach. The fresh air would do Marlene good.

A large WOMEN ON BOARD banner was being pulled behind a small commercial plane through the clouds. Another WOMEN ON BOARD sign stood in the sand about three hundred feet south of the pavilion.

About a dozen teenage girls lay on surfboards in the sand near the sign.

Mary Frances had said that classes began today and the

course would run for three weeks. Of course, Roberto wouldn't be here this afternoon; he'd be tangoing with Mary Frances, but Claude might have started working.

Kate slipped out of her sandals and rolled up her khakis. Marlene, dressed in a flowing red top worn over white Capris, struggled with the laces on her espadrilles.

They trudged through the hot sand toward the girls.

"Try those pop-ups again." Their instructor, a tall, sturdy brunette in her early thirties, spoke in a pleasant tone but with great authority. "Find your inner Gidget."

The girls, as instructed, tried to stand and balance on their boards. Not easy to do, even out of the water. Most of them tumbled into the sand amid great laughter. It wouldn't seem as funny when they tumbled into a huge wave.

"Hey," Marlene said, staring at the ocean. Kate, too, spotted Claude Jensen, standing waist deep in the water, talking to a pretty, young blonde who was lying on a surfboard, paddling as he spoke.

Sweating and puffing, Kate approached the tall brunette. She'd make sure Claude had taught his last lesson at the surfing camp and that Roberto would never teach his first

Thirty-Three

"That dreadful Detective Carbone asked—well, *ordered*—Mom to fly back from Asia." Her granddaughter Lauren's indignation resonated in Kate's ear. Her cell phone, when she remembered to carry it, was at best a mixed blessing. "Mom can't get a flight until this evening, Nana, and it's very convoluted. She'll have to fly to Istanbul, then to Frankfurt, then to JFK, and then to Fort Lauderdale."

Kate and Marlene were driving north on A1A. They'd just passed what had to be the best Best Western in America. The inn was located on the beach, just north of the Marriott Harbor Beach, an elegant, very expensive high-rise hotel.

"Mom kept this mess from Daddy for as long as she could, but he and I are flying down to Florida tomorrow. I think Carbone likes Mom for Grace Rowling's murder, but not for Jon Michael's shark attack," Lauren, pre-law at Harvard, said. "Nana, how could Katharine have gotten herself involved with that low-life surfer? It's ruining my fall break, not to mention my parents' careers."

Ah yes, Lauren Kennedy had inherited her mother's Lowell genes.

Kate hated to admit it, even to herself, but she wasn't looking forward to having her family descend on Palmetto Beach. Their presence would only complicate her investigation.

"I don't believe your mother is a suspect. I'm sure Detective Carbone just wants to clear up some issues," Kate said, conveying more confidence than she felt. Why hadn't Jennifer mentioned that Monday night post-dinner visit to Grace's room? A lie of omission, as the nuns would have said. There had to be several lies of omission in this case; they were always much more difficult to detect than blatant lies.

"Whatever," Lauren said, without enthusiasm. "Nana, Mom had her secretary book two rooms at the Boca Raton Hotel, so you won't have us all underfoot. We'll see you soon. Oh, and Daddy sends his love." Lauren hung up before Kate could respond.

"More company coming?" Marlene's low chuckle sounded rueful.

"The only ones who'll be missing are Peter and Edmund, and I wouldn't take book on their not showing up." Kate sighed. "At least Kevin and Lauren will be staying up in Boca. Jennifer too, when she arrives."

"What about Katharine?"

If anyone had asked Kate before this very minute if she loved all her children and grandchildren equally, she'd have answered yes, and she'd have meant it. Marlene's question made Kate realize that answer wouldn't have been the truth. She wanted Katharine to stay with her because Katharine was special, a sweet down-to-earth girl who reminded Kate of Charlie. And yes, she loved Katharine, if not more, then differently from the way she loved the others. Hell, she loved Marlene, with all her faults, more than she loved Jennifer. And, if she should feel guilty or disloyal, she didn't.

"Katharine will stay with me," her grandmother said. This time Marlene's chuckle sounded knowing.

They drove for a while in silence, rare for the old friends, unless one of them was angry. A view of the Reef finally broke that silence.

The Palmetto Beach city fathers had voted to approve the huge, luxurious—the builder's adjective, not Kate's—condominium, built in the southernmost part of the city on two adjoining lots, after the city had razed the perfectly fine condos that had been standing on those lots since the sixties.

The Reef's sales brochure proclaimed its condo dwellers would "live like royalty, submerged in elegance." The glossy promo also pointed out that trendy boutiques, entertaining hot spots, and diving excursions were available in Boca Raton, Palm Beach, and Fort Lauderdale—not mentioning that the city of Palmetto Beach had none of those amenities.

The condos ranged from $1.6 to $5 million. With the real estate boom over, the Reef now had a glut of unsold luxury.

"Mary Frances told me Joe Sajak bought a two-bedroom condo there on spec, putting down ten percent, figuring he could turn it around for a fast profit," Marlene said. "Now he's crying foul, threatening to sue the builder. Says the Italian marble in the kitchen is fake."

Kate's chuckle was neither rueful nor knowing. She was just plain tickled.

"Well, if Joe can't unload it, maybe he'll have to sell his Ocean Vista condo and move to the Reef. You should have been nicer to him, Marlene."

"Maybe you can walk the rest of the way home."

Lauderdale-by-the-Sea had a building code prohibiting high-rises and preserving the city's charm. In Palmetto Beach, low-rise apartment houses and motels, dwarfed by taller neighbors, sometimes went unnoticed.

Kate almost missed the Crest. "Whoa, Marlene, quick, make a right here. That's the motel where Roberto Romero lives." She pointed to a New England-style clapboard cottage, complete with trellis and rosebushes. Its back door had to exit into the sand dunes.

"You'd think they'd have a sign bigger than a postage stamp," Marlene said. "And where are we supposed to park?"

"I don't think they're looking for customers. I bet the Crest doesn't advertise; that's why we never heard of it. And if you didn't know about it, you'd drive right by."

The six-car parking lot was full, but Kate saw no black Cadillac among the Lexus and Mercedes rentals.

"Why don't you go in, Kate? I'll park by the front door and stay in the car. It doesn't look like there's much happening here."

Kate scrambled out of the car before Marlene changed her mind.

The Wedgwood blue door opened into a room decorated with chintz loveseats and mahogany tables and smelling of lemon-scented furniture polish.

Kate felt as if she'd left Palmetto Beach behind and stepped into Nantucket.

A sandy-haired young man wearing a white shirt and gold-and-blue-striped school tie sat at campaign desk; its top held a leather-bound registration book but no computer.

"May I help you, madam?" Why wasn't she surprised that he had a Mid-Atlantic accent?

"I'm looking for Roberto Romero. I understand he lives

here," she said, praying her quarry wouldn't walk in and catch her.

"That is no longer the case, madam, and I can give you no other information, unless, of course, you're with the police." He almost snickered.

Kate, noting her rolled-up khakis and old sandals, could hardly blame him.

So Nick Carbone had beaten her to the Crest. Had the snooty young clerk been more cooperative with the homicide detective?

Feeling dejected and resentful, she waked out into the late-afternoon sunshine and found Marlene in animated conversation with an elderly gardener who was watering the rosebushes. Could that be a twenty-dollar bill Marlene just pressed into his free hand?

Kate stayed to their right, blatantly eavesdropping.

"He smokes Cuban cigars and drinks Johnnie Walker on the rocks," the old man was telling Marlene. Her sister-in-law nodded encouragingly. "Romero's a real big tipper. He don't stay here all the time. I hear he has some old dame down in Miami. Like I told that homicide detective, I think Romero's green card's a fake. But for an illegal alien, that young man sure lives well and dates some real beauties. A regular Latin lover. No visible means of support." The gardener turned his hose off. "Did you say the story would be in *People*?"

"Week after next," Marlene lied, handing the man another twenty. She glanced over at Kate. "Meet my editor."

Thirty-Four

"You should have been an actress," Kate said as they walked into the Ocean Vista lobby. "Your lies sound so smooth, so scripted."

"What kind of a crack is that?" Marlene snapped.

"It's not a crack." Kate heard the edge of anger in her own voice too. "I'm grateful, that's all; you pulled off what I couldn't."

"Well, you thanked me twice in the car." Marlene, not mollified, sounded like a spoiled child. What was behind her sister-in-law's behavior? Certainly not what had happened in front of the Crest Motel or on their way home, but Kate didn't feel up to examining issues from their past. They had enough to deal with in the present.

Several of their fellow condo owners were taking down the Halloween balloons and orange and black crepe paper. They'd been up for less than thirty hours. Miss Mitford stood behind her desk, overseeing with her usual disdain. Kate winced when she saw several boxes marked CHRISTMAS DECORATIONS.

"This would have never happened on my watch," Marlene said.

"You ran a tight condo," Kate said, making Marlene smile. A real smile, letting Kate know everything was okay again.

"Hey, Marlene," a voice called from behind Aphrodite. "I've been waiting for you."

Sam Meyers walked around the fountain. He must have been sitting on the other side of the lobby, watching the decorations being dismantled.

If Marlene was as surprised as Kate to see Sam in their lobby, she didn't show it. "Hello, Sam," she said, all full of charm. "Do you remember my sister-in-law, Kate Kennedy? You met her briefly at Dinah's last night."

"Hi, Kate," Sam said, and then stared over at the cupids. "Er, look, ladies, I'm here because Katharine called me." He seemed agitated, checking his watch. "We have a date in fifteen minutes. She wants me to go with her to visit Jon Michael's grandmother, you know, like a condolence call."

"I thought you hardly knew Katharine," Marlene said. "You told me she'd left Acapulco before you arrived there."

"Yeah, that's right," Sam stammered. "I surfed with her here a couple of times, though, and hung with her and the other boardsmen at the Neptune Inn."

Kate thought he was lying, but about what?

"I'm down with taking Katharine," Sam said. "Here's the problem: I can't go to see Florita Flannigan with Katharine unless Annette comes too. She's off addressing the Fort Lauderdale NOW chapter, Marlene, telling them how proud they all should be of you, what a wonderful advocate you were for her cause."

Kate bit her lip as Marlene blanched.

"Annette is very possessive, but she trusts you, Marlene. The only way Katharine and I can visit Florita is if you'll join us." Sam, having spoken his piece, seemed to relax.

"Then, afterward, we all can have dinner at the Neptune Inn."

"Well, Sam, I have a problem too," Marlene said. "Florita is royally ticked off at me. I had a run-in with her talking skull, and I assure you I wouldn't be welcome at her house again."

"On the other hand," Kate said, smiling in what she hoped was a grandmotherly fashion, "Florita likes me. She even gave me a discount when I consulted with Mandrake. May I be your chaperone, Sam?"

He nodded, not unlike an eager puppy.

"Okay, I'll freshen up, collect Katharine, and we'll be ready to roll. Marlene will make reservations for all of us except herself at the Neptune Inn. Now, Sam, please relax. Or help take down the Halloween decorations. Or chat with Miss Mitford at the front desk; she's quite the Palmetto Beach historian. Katharine and I will be down in less than ten minutes."

As they stepped into the elevator, Marlene said, "I know I can't go to Florita's house, but why can't I go to the Neptune Inn?"

"Because not only is Florita Flannigan mad as hell at you, Annette Meyers is about to discover that you are not now and never were a card-carrying member of NOW." Kate pressed three. "I need to talk to you while I'm getting ready. Marlene, can't you see, this is an unexpected opportunity? I'll be spending the evening with our two prime suspects for Diamond Lil. And I need your input about Annette beforehand."

"What will I do when you're out playing detective?" Kate heard the pout in Marlene's voice.

"Don't worry, I have an assignment for you. One you won't be able to refuse."

"It better be more exciting than my last assignment," Marlene said as they exited the elevator. "No more stupid research. I'm a people person."

"Right," Kate agreed, remembering how Florita Flannigan had branded Marlene "unstable."

"You do know Sam Meyers is full of it, don't you?" Marlene followed Kate down the hall. "Annette told me Sam's the jealous one. His 'granny' believes in open relationships like the one she's enjoying with that good-looking Navy guy. So why would Annette be jealous if Sam and Katharine went to Florita's without a bloody chaperone?"

"Maybe what's good for the gander isn't good for the goose." Kate giggled.

Marlene groaned. "That's so bad, I won't even comment."

Kate stopped a few feet away from her door. "This is just a hunch. I have no proof and it makes no sense…"

"And when has lack of proof or lack of sanity ever stopped us?" As she had for decades, Marlene made Kate feel better.

"Okay, here goes. I think Diamond Lil is connected to these murders. I don't know how or why; I just do."

Marlene nodded. "And you believe either Annette or Florita might be Diamond Lil?"

"Yes, though based on what I glimpsed on the television at Dinah's, Florita's eyes aren't quite right. I'm going to check out Annette's eyes tonight."

"What can I do to help?" Marlene sounded excited.

"I want you and Mary Frances to find out the name and address of Roberto's patroness and where she lives in Miami. Then you and I will go visit her tomorrow. Any woman who sleeps in her jewels might well be Diamond Lil."

Thirty-Five

"Sex on the beach." Sam sounded impatient. It was clear that Herb, Kate's good friend and the owner of the Neptune Inn, had never heard of the drink Sam had ordered.

"I'm sure my regular bartender would know, but I'm on my own here tonight," Herb said. "So what else besides vodka and schnapps goes into the shaker?"

"A shot of vodka, a shot of peach schnapps, two shots of cranberry juice, and a splash of pineapple juice," Sam said. "That's the way they make it on Oahu's north shore. Oahu's awesome. The best surfing in Hawaii, the best swells in the world, and the best sex on the beach too."

"I'll try to live up to Oahu's standards," Herb said, reaching for a cocktail shaker. "The Neptune Inn aims to please."

Florita had not only accepted the dinner invitation, she'd been waiting outside at her front gate when Sam, Katharine, and Kate, the *duenna*, had picked her up.

Now the four of them were sitting at the Neptune Inn's bar waiting for Annette to arrive.

"I'll have a sex on the beach too," Florita said. "Sure beats white wine, doesn't it?" For a grandmother in mourning, she seemed to be enjoying herself.

Kate said, "I'd like a Diet Coke."

"Me too," Katharine said. The girl had been very quiet, too quiet, in the car both going to and coming from Florita's.

"Where else have you surfed, Sam?" Kate asked. She'd been under the impression Sam was a computer geek who hadn't spent much time riding the waves. But then, she'd also thought he hadn't been in Acapulco and she'd been wrong about that.

"Black's Beach in San Diego. Sweet, man. It has one of the best reefs in the world. And just last June I went to Lahinch in Ireland. Way wild surfing there. We were towed by Jet Skis to just below the Cliffs of Moher. We had to wear wet suits, gloves, and boots in that damn cold water, but the waves were totally awesome."

Where had Sam gotten the money to surf around the world? Maybe Granny Meyers wasn't the first older woman he'd "loved." Or maybe the surfboard smuggling operation hadn't been so small; maybe Sam had been part of it.

"I'm of Irish descent, you know," Florita Flannigan said. "So I plan to have a proper send-off for Jon Michael." She sipped her sex on the beach; Herb had served her first. "I thought we were meeting tonight to talk about his wake and the funeral." She turned to Sam. "No disrespect to you, but my grandson died surfing. I'm sick of hearing about what a wonderful sport it is."

Kate, the instigator, felt a wave of shame wash over her. She, not Sam, had been guilty of gross insensitivity. Again, she wondered why Katharine had called Sam. Hadn't her granddaughter believed she could count on Kate to drive her to Florita's? One thing was clear: Katharine hadn't wanted to go there alone.

"Please forgive me, Florita." Kate didn't have to feign regret; her sincerity was real. "That's why we're here. How can Katharine and I help?"

Katharine smiled at her grandmother. The warmth in her granddaughter's eyes moved Kate. She'd been afraid the girl she loved so deeply could have been lost to her forever. Tonight, planning a funeral for the boy who'd broken Katharine's heart might bring Kate and her granddaughter back together.

Florita toyed with the three-strand pearl choker that encircled the turtleneck of her black silk dress. If those were real pearls, they had to have cost a fortune. Kate tried to focus on Florita's eyes, but in the dimly lit bar, she couldn't see much of anything.

"Well, Detective Carbone tells me they'll release Jon Michael's body by tomorrow afternoon. I want to have the requiem mass in Hollywood."

"California?" Sam asked. "That seems like a long way to travel to a funeral."

Florita flicked her wrist in the surfer's direction, but continued to address Kate and Katharine, who sat to her right.

"The mission church, down in Hollywood, the one with the grotto, where they reenact the passion and the crucifixion every Holy Week."

Kate, the church-hopper, nodded. "I just love Father Sean's sermons."

"And I thought we'd hold the wake at home. Mandrake

doesn't like to go out, you know, and his shrine is really a chapel anyway."

Even Kate, a veteran of hundreds of Irish wakes, was stumped.

"I thought we'd have the wake Friday night and the requiem mass and burial on Saturday." Florita finished her drink and gestured toward Herb for another. "How does that sound?" she asked of no one in particular, though she patted Katharine's knee.

"Great," Katharine said. "I'll be glad to help buy the food for the wake and help serve it." She touched Kate's hand. "You'll help too, won't you, Nana?"

Sensing closure—and what did that word really mean?—keeping busy at the wake and funeral would help her granddaughter. Kate said, "Of course. Whatever I can do."

"Well, I thought the wake could be potluck," Florita said. "You know, all the mourners could bring a covered dish or a cake. Do you bake, Kate?"

"No, I buy," a stunned Kate said. "But Dinah's has delicious cakes and pies. I'll take care of dessert."

"I guess I could bring a couple of six-packs," Sam offered. Florita clapped her hands. "There we go. And so many of Mandrake's clients have volunteered to bring food, I think we'll be just fine. Jon Michael will have a proper send-off." She turned to Herb, who smiled at Florita with respect and concern. "I know my grandson and his friends spent a lot of time here, Herb. Do you think the Neptune Inn could donate a couple of cases of wine?"

Herb, a gentle giant of a man, never blinked. "How about two cases of red and two white?"

Kate, who'd gone from sympathy to outrage, had heard enough. "That's really much too generous, Herb."

"Yes, indeed," Florita said. "One case of red and one of white would be just fine. Maybe a robust merlot, and make the white champagne. Cristal would be wonderful."

Herb shook his head, jowls swinging. "The Neptune Inn doesn't stock fine champagnes, Florita. I'll send the best we have."

"Good, then we're all set except for the video."

Dear God, what now? Kate's jaw hadn't been this tight in over thirty years.

"What video?" Sam asked.

"Mandrake suggested that I immortalize Jon Michael. So I found a way to make sure his voice will be heard from the grave." Florita's smile moved from Kate to Katharine to Sam. "I'm putting his eulogy, our family albums, his videos with those glorious surfing shots, and the newspaper clippings and photos of Jon Michael singing country western on a quarter-sized computer memory device that will be embedded in his tombstone. My grandson's mourners will be able activate a medallion on the front of his tombstone with some sort of magic wand and retrieve Jon Michael's life story, and then display it on a laptop computer. And the Palmetto Beach Cemetery has agreed to provide handheld computers and those wands to all of Jon Michael's visitors in perpetuity."

"Cool," Sam said. "Righteous. Can Annette and I videotape a good-bye message?"

"Certainly," Florita said. "Everyone will be taping their farewells at the wake."

Katharine stared down at the floor and said nothing. Kate figured Florita would take up a collection at the funeral to pay for Jon Michael's immortality.

"I'm here," Annette Meyers called out as she made her way through the crowd at the bar.

Kate's glance moved from the diamond brooch on Annette's lapel up to her diamond earrings and over to her glowing eyes. Whatever vagary Kate had been searching for, she didn't find.

Thirty-Six

Thursday morning, November 2

Where was Katharine? She'd said she'd meet Kate at St. John's, insisting that she had to light a candle and say a prayer for her grandfather on All Souls' Day, and now she hadn't shown up.

Mass had ended five minutes ago and the church was eerily empty. Kate could hear the laughter of children drifting across the trellised walkway that separated the school from the church.

She knelt in front of the statue of the Blessed Virgin, staring at an array of blazing candles that would delight a pyromaniac.

Should she leave? Go back to Ocean Vista? She'd tried Katharine's cell phone, but hadn't even reached her voicemail. Odd, but maybe the batteries were dead, if cell phones had batteries. What Kate didn't know about technology would fill the Manhattan phone book.

She lit two candles to honor her granddaughter's intentions and then stood up. Her left knee creaked. Growing old was a pain.

Lauren and Kevin would be landing in Fort Lauderdale at five. She couldn't waste any more time. Kate needed this case wrapped up before she met that plane.

Sunshine bathed the courtyard adjacent to the walkway and the parking lot. Kate could hear sweet young voices, maybe first graders, singing "Puff, the Magic Dragon." A nun on the walkway to the school waved. Kate waved back and then slid into her car, deciding she had no choice but to go back home.

She smelled his cologne before he spoke.

"I hope you remembered me in your prayers, señora." Roberto hid on the floor of the backseat behind her.

"How...?"

"I have been busy while you were at mass. As a result of my labor, your granddaughter is tied up at the moment, but looking forward to seeing you."

Kate twisted her head, her pulse rate up so high, her heart felt as if it might explode.

"Don't turn around. I have a gun aimed up at your straw hat. Now, *por favor,* Señora Kennedy, drive down A1A toward Miami."

Kate pulled out of the church driveway and headed south.

She'd contacted an immigration official just before she'd left for church. He'd promised they'd talk to Roberto and find out if he had papers. One of her mother's favorite axioms popped into Kate's head: a day late and a dollar short.

But she had to do something. Say something. "You're here illegally, Roberto. You came in a boat, didn't you, to find freedom? If you let Katharine and me go. I'll help you get a green card."

"Nice try, señora. The US government doesn't give green cards to smugglers. Even to brave ones who surfed from a fishing boat anchored many miles offshore to reach America."

"What did you smuggle?" Kate felt doomed, but wouldn't stop trying. She had to find a way to save Katharine.

Roberto laughed. "First I smuggled me." Though Kate couldn't see him, she pictured his flashing eyes and white teeth. "Then with Jon Michael, I smuggled cigars, pot, and sometimes cocaine." He sounded proud, as if he were describing an achievement listed on his resume.

"Under the surfboard? In wire baskets, holding waterproof bags?" Kate spoke without thinking.

"You're a sharp old lady." Roberto sounded strained, angry.

Kate shut up. She'd said too much. Her heart throbbed and her mind whirled. Wire mesh baskets of some sort had been attached to the bottom of Roberto's and Jon Michael's surfboards and used to transport cigars and cocaine from Cuban fishing boats to Palmetto Beach's shore. A falling out among the smugglers must have led Roberto to put pig's blood into one of the waterproof bags—with a deliberate slow leak—knowing the blood would attract sharks to Jon Michael's board.

They drove in silence from Fort Lauderdale to Hollywood, until A1A veered away from the ocean.

"Turn left on the next corner." Roberto had broken the silence, barking an order. "Make a quick right and pull into the Casablanca Motel."

The faded motel, with a hint of Middle Eastern

architecture, had seen better days. In its heyday, the location, across a narrow street from sand, must have been a great draw. Now the windows were boarded and a FOR SALE sign had been stuck in the neglected lawn.

October was still off-season, but a few tourists, all staring out at the sea, were on the beach. There were no other cars in sight.

Roberto jabbed the gun into Kate's right shoulder. "Get out."

Kate slipped and her wedges sank down into the sandy ground, making walking difficult. She kicked her shoes off, bent quickly to pick them up, and caught sight of another motel, only yards away. Was it open? Should she make a run for it? Or scream? Not without Katharine. Not with Roberto out of the car and the gun in her ribcage.

A biker passed by and waved. "*Vaya con dios*," Roberto called out.

Kate was convinced she could kill Romero without a qualm of conscience.

Thirty-Seven

Marlene and Mary Frances, like *Thelma & Louise*—well, maybe Marlene should rethink that comparison since the movie hadn't had a happy ending—were on a road trip to Miami.

Last night Marlene had reached out to Mary Frances, who'd agreed to help track down Roberto's Miami girlfriend, saying, "I've always been jealous of you and Kate having all the fun."

In a bit of brilliant detective work, Mary Frances had swiped Roberto's cell phone when he'd gone to the men's room in Dinah's. She immediately went to the ladies room and jotted down every number in the 305 area code Roberto had programmed into his speed dial. When she returned to the table, she said, "Isn't that your cell phone on the floor, Roberto?" As she spoke, she bent down, slipped his phone out of her hand and onto the floor, then made a big show of picking it up and handing it to him.

Every once in a while it crossed Marlene's mind that maybe, just maybe, she could be friends with Mary Frances.

That feeling was often fleeting. But today, with the convertible top down, the sun at their back, and Roberto's lady friend's address tucked in Mary Frances's handbag—the dancing nun had made four calls before connecting with Roberto's patroness—Marlene was reconsidering.

"I never knew you spoke Spanish," Marlene said.

Mary Frances sighed. "There's a lot you don't know about me, Marlene. Early in my career as a nun, I taught for four years in a mission school in El Salvador. I speak Spanish as well as I do French and Sudanese."

"Sudanese?"

"Forty years ago, I served as a peace corps volunteer in Africa. I almost left the convent for a doctor, but his people needed him more than he needed me."

"That's too bad." Marlene meant what she said. She might even grow to like Mary Frances.

"It's okay. I think the good doctor loved my red hair more than he loved me. There aren't a lot of redheads in the Sudan."

"Jon Michael didn't like Katharine's red hair. He said some cruel things to her."

"All of the boardsmen have a mean streak. Jon Michael had one too. Any of them could have murdered that missing girl, Amanda Rowling. Roberto said Jon Michael had told Amanda when they'd all been at the bar in Acapulco that he'd take her surfing and give her the ride of her life. It wouldn't have been Jon Michael's first midnight ride, but maybe it was Amanda's last." Mary Frances pushed windswept hair off her face. "And the señora in Miami seems to have decided that Roberto isn't her Prince Charming after all."

"But she didn't tell you anything specific, right?" Marlene asked for at least the tenth time.

"No. You know what I know." Mary Frances laughed. "When I told Sylvia I was Roberto's dancing partner and I had serious questions about his means of support, his lifestyle, and immigration status, she'd replied with the Spanish equivalent of 'come on down.'"

"We have to be back by four o'clock. I'm going to the airport with Kate and Katharine to pick up my nephew, Kevin—he was named after my second husband—and my grandniece, Lauren." Marlene spoke with pride. Childless and husbandless she might be, but she had family, by marriage to be sure, but still family.

Thirty minutes later they'd reached Miami and Mary Frances hadn't run out of Costellos. After having heard about every one of Mary Frances's hundreds of relatives, living and dead, the bloody family tree back to the Civil War, Marlene seriously regretted her bragging.

Sylvia Vargas lived on Key Biscayne. Driving across the long, elegant bridge connecting the key to the mainland, Marlene marveled at the beauty of Miami, both the city's natural beauty, the water and the palm trees, and its manmade beauty, the magnificent skyline.

"That's Bayview Drive," Mary Frances said, looking up from her directions. "We turn left here." The very organized former teacher, nun, and Peace Corps volunteer had pulled up the directions on MapQuest.

There were two houses in the cul-de-sac; both were magnificent, old Florida moss-covered mansions. But only one had a police car parked in front of it.

Mary Frances and Marlene wouldn't be speaking to Sylvia Vargas. Someone had slit her throat.

Thirty-Eight

Roberto had a key. He opened the arched door to the motel and pushed Kate through ahead of him. They entered a dingy and damp reception area smelling of mildew.

"Down that hallway." Roberto gestured to the right. They passed several closed doors and then came to an open one. "Go on in," he said, and followed her into a room with an ocean view and peeling wallpaper featuring faded flamingoes.

The room was square, with two double beds, an old-fashioned highboy dresser, two end tables, a desk, a straight-back desk chair, a wicker coffee table, and two small club chairs. A black phone, circa 1960, stood on one of the end tables, evoking old New York memories of Pennsylvania 6 and Butterfield 8. Roberto drew the tattered camel-colored drapes and the daylight ebbed.

Roberto opened another door and motioned Kate over.

She shook her head, standing pat. He charged at her, knocking her straw hat off, and then dragged her by the collar of her white polo shirt into the closet.

"Please," Kate cried, the tears hot against her cheeks.

"Where's Katharine?"

"I'm moving the car around to the back. Your granddaughter will be joining you soon. Now the señora will shut up if she knows what's good for her." He shut the closet door and she heard a key turn in the lock.

The Casablanca had been built more than fifty years ago. Kate couldn't budge the solid oak door. The smell of mothballs turned her stomach sour. Her Pepcid AC was in her bag and she'd left her bag in the car. She bit her lip to keep from screaming. Would anyone hear her? Would she die in here? Was Katharine already dead?

She sank to her knees, saying a prayer.

It was too dark in the closet to see her watch, but Kate felt certain several hours had passed. She was thirsty and her bladder felt full. Panic ebbed as cold terror took over, settling into her chest, eating at her gut.

Sitting with her back against a wall, listening to bugs—roaches—scurry in the dark, she'd about given up, sure she would die in this god-awful closet without knowing if her granddaughter was dead or alive. Then she heard the sound of a woman's laughter.

She forced herself to stand up and pounded on the door, screaming, "Let me out of here!"

The light in the room hurt Kate's eyes as Roberto held the closet door open. "Come out and join us, señora."

Katharine lay still on the twin bed nearest the window. Her skin was ashen.

"What have you done to her?" Kate shouted, and then darted across the room to Katharine's bedside.

Her granddaughter's breathing seemed normal and, other than lack of color, there was no visible harm to her body. Kate's panic grew. Why wasn't Katharine moving?

Kate took Katharine's hand and said, "Darling, it's Nana, can you hear me?"

The girl wore the same clothes she'd been wearing this morning when she'd walked Ballou, a pale green t-shirt and olive green baggy khakis. Her black patent leather flip-flops lay, as if waiting for Katharine to step back into them, on the floor at the bottom of the bed. The sight of those flip-flops had turned Kate's terror to anger.

"I want you to tell me what you did to her," Kate said. Her voice was icy, but not loud. "Answer me!"

Roberto shrugged. "She's fine, just sleeping off a tranquilizer. Now sit down and shut up, Señora Kennedy, or I promise you will regret it. We have a plan to make and a script to memorize."

Kate needed to buy time, make a plan of her own, but first things first. "Roberto, I need water and I need to use the bathroom. Now."

She looked around the room. There was no sign of the laughing woman. Who was she and where had she gone?

Thirty-Nine

"Ransom?" Marlene's hysteria came through loud and clear on Roberto's cell phone's speaker. "God Almighty! Are you okay? Is Katharine okay?"

Kate sat in one of the dirty chintz club chairs facing Roberto, who sat in the matching chair less than a foot away from her. They had put Roberto's plan into action.

Kate, afraid to utter an unscripted word, glanced over at Roberto. He nodded.

"Yes, we're okay." Kate felt weird to be talking without a phone in her hand, and even weirder to be having this conversion.

"How much?" Marlene asked, not sounding the least bit reassured. "And where do I bring the money?"

With her eyes on her sleeping granddaughter, Kate, heart pounding, delivered her next line exactly as rehearsed with Roberto. "Clean out your CD, the one with Katharine as your beneficiary at the SunTrust Bank in Palmetto Beach. Get a cashier's check made out to Katharine Kennedy."

Marlene Friedman's third and last husband, Jack Weiss,

had been a very successful man, and his widow was now a wealthy woman. Marlene's estate would be divided among Kate, Katharine, and Lauren, though Kate had always hoped that she would die before her best friend. If Roberto had his way, she might get her wish.

Lovesick women do foolish things. Katharine had told Jon Michael about her grandaunt's bank account. Roberto had overheard, and the seeds of his sick plan had been planted, becoming one of several motives for Jon Michael's death.

She wanted to reach over and touch Katharine. The girl looked so ill. So vulnerable. What kind of drug had that bastard given her? Could her granddaughter be in a coma?

Roberto's plan had included using Katharine's ID to cash the cashier's check. Kate knew once that transaction was completed, Katharine and Kate would become expendable.

The plan also called for Roberto to hang up as soon as Kate had given Marlene the money transfer instructions. She had to do something now. Send some sort of a signal to Marlene.

"Where are you?" Marlene asked, her hysteria on hold.

Roberto shook his head.

"I can't tell you where I am."

"Can the kidnapper hear me?"

"Yes." Kate watched Roberto's face. "He can hear you." She took a deep breath, and then spoke. "Listen very carefully to what I'm telling you."

Kate was about to insert her first ad-lib. Would Roberto notice?

"As time goes by, you must remember this." She paused. Roberto's expression hadn't changed. She might be able to pull this off, and then pray Marlene had gotten the message.

Kate continued, "For the sake of our beautiful friendship," she paused again for less than a second, and said, "you must understand what I'm saying and do everything I'm trying to tell you. If you don't, Katharine will be killed."

"Go on, Kate." Marlene sounded almost calm.

"Be at SunTrust tomorrow morning when it opens at eight. When you leave the bank, a woman will approach you. An older woman. Give her the cashier's check, then get in your car and drive home. Don't talk to the police or discuss this call with anyone."

Roberto nodded, indicating Kate should wrap it up.

"You must remember what I told you. Otherwise we'll both regret it for the rest of our lives. You've always understood when I tried to tell you something important, Marlene. I'm counting on that now." Kate didn't dare look at Roberto.

"I understand," Marlene said.

Kate prayed she did.

"Dinner's here." A woman's voice shouted from the hall.

Roberto leapt from his chair and opened the door.

An old lady, balancing two pizza boxes and a six-pack of Diet Coke, entered. She wore a lavender sweat suit and her perfectly coiffed hair looked like a wig. Huge diamonds dangled from her earlobes, neck, and wrist.

Roberto's face sparkled like the old lady's jewels. As Marlene had said, lots of odd couples in this case.

Kate checked out the woman's eyes. Yes! She was about to meet Diamond Lil. Damn. Where had she seen those eyes before?

Katharine stirred, then woke up crying.

Kate ran over and held her granddaughter close, murmuring. "It's okay. Everything will be okay, darling."

"Nana, I'm so sorry. He grabbed me after Marlene dropped me off at church. I tried to scream, but I couldn't. He put something over my face and shoved me in the trunk." Katharine sobbed. "No one saw us, Nana. The parking lot was empty."

"It's okay," Kate said again. Why did she keep saying that when everything was so wrong?

"Stop crying, Katharine," Roberto said. "We all want to enjoy our dinner, don't we?"

As Diamond Lil served the pizza, Kate noticed her hands. Nary a vein, a sunspot, or a dry patch. Not an old lady's hands. They were the smooth, tanned-to-perfection hands of a teenage girl.

Forty

Friday morning, November 3

This could be the last day of my life, Kate thought as she awoke from a fitful sleep in the chintz chair. The last day of Katharine's life. She remained still, her eyes closed, fighting an urge to check on her granddaughter. She didn't want her kidnappers to know she was awake. *Kidnap.* What a strange verb to describe such a horrific crime. Children weren't the only ones abducted, grabbed off the street, taken from their beds, and held against their will. Kate, a senior citizen, and Katharine, a college student, had been *kidnapped. Kidnap* was a misnomer.

Murder, on the other hand, was an all-inclusive verb. Kate felt helpless, frightened. She no longer had control over her destiny; she could only pray Marlene had gotten her message. She asked St. Jude to give her strength. And maybe a small miracle.

"Wake up," Roberto said as he shook her shoulder. Kate opened her eyes and glanced at her watch. Six thirty. Beyond those drawn drapes, the sun was coming up and early risers, with freedom of choice, had started their day.

Six thirty. If Marlene had understood Kate's message, the police should have been here by now. Had she seen her last sunrise? An inner voice scolded: get hold of yourself. Don't give up.

Katharine snored softly. Kate's fear was replaced with anger as she stared at her granddaughter. She turned to Roberto. "What did you give her?"

He shrugged, seeming to realize that whatever he told Kate wouldn't matter if his plan worked, and he was arrogant enough to be sure it would. "Equal parts Tylenol PM and water."

God, when help arrived, she'd take Katharine to the hospital. Kate smiled, and a small giggle escaped: she'd thought *when,* not if.

"Something is funny, señora?"

"An inside joke, Roberto."

The bathroom door opened and a beautiful young redhead in white shorts, a t-shirt, and no shoes walked out.

Amanda Rowling, the missing co-ed, was alive and well, and Roberto's partner in crime. She had her mother's eyes.

Amanda must have dyed her hair red so she could pass for Katharine when she cashed Marlene's cashier's check for over $350,000. She'd have Katharine's driver's license, student ID, and credit cards. Kate had spotted her granddaughter's handbag on the bureau.

"Would you like a cup of tea, Kate?" the girl asked, and then poured boiling water from an ancient coffeemaker into two mugs.

Kate sipped her tea, watching in silent, sick fascination as Amanda transformed herself into Diamond Lil.

Grace Rowling had told Kate what a great actress her daughter was. She was also a great makeup artist, using gray eye shadow to create dark bags and the illusion of wrinkles. She even used cotton balls to make her face fatter. Roberto taped pillows to her breasts, buttocks, and thighs. Dark tights covered those slim, tanned legs. When Amanda pulled on her frumpy housedress, she looked lumpy in all the right—or wrong—places. She stepped into Dr. Scholl's sandals, winking at Kate. She adjusted her white wig and topped it with a tiara. Her transformation was complete. Amanda Rowling had become Diamond Lil.

Kissing Roberto on the cheek, she pushed him away as he tried for her lips. "Stop, you'll mess up my makeup." They both laughed at what had to be their private joke. "I'll call you when I'm on my way back."

Diamond Lil left the Casablanca Motel at seven fifteen, allowing more than enough time to arrive in Palmetto Beach by eight.

If Roberto's plan worked, and Amanda got the check and cashed it on her way back to the motel, Kate figured she and Katharine had about an hour and a half to live.

Kate sat in the dirty chintz chair, trying to disappear into its flowers.

Katharine slept and neither Roberto nor Kate spoke.

At eight fifteen, Roberto, the gun in his shirt pocket, paced as Kate boiled water to make a cup of tea for Katharine. The girl had awakened about five minutes ago and had heeded her grandmother's index finger to her lip as a signal to keep quiet.

Amanda could be calling any minute, authorizing Katharine and Kate's death warrant.

Kate poured the hot water into a mug. Should she try to

grab the gun? Yell for Katharine to run and save herself? Kate had to try. Now.

Something crashed through the widow facing the beach. The drapes billowed and then parted, revealing a man's arm. Behind Kate and Roberto, the door made a wheezing sound, then burst open.

Roberto swung around, aiming the gun at Kate. She threw the hot water in his face as Katharine screamed and Nick Carbone yelled, "Freeze!"

Marlene had gotten the message.

Epilogue

Saturday morning, November 4

"Kate, did you know the police checked out one hotel, two restaurants, and three motels in Broward and Dade Counties, all called Casablanca?" Marlene held up her mimosa. "A toast to classic movies and their great dialogue."

"Yes, Nick told me." Kate smiled at the detective who sat to her right. "And I'd thought there was only one *Casablanca*."

Kevin and Jennifer had insisted on hosting a brunch at the Boca Raton Hotel to celebrate Kate and Katharine's safe return.

Katharine had told Kate, "Mom wants to make nice with Detective Carbone."

They were sitting on the hotel's elegant terrace, being served delicious food on beautiful china, sipping drinks from crystal glasses, and watching a surfer trying to catch a wave in the aquamarine water of the Atlantic Ocean.

"And I understand the police arrested Amanda in the SunTrust parking lot," Kate said.

"That was such fun," Marlene said. "I handed her an empty envelope and they carted her off: Her white wig fell off."

Katharine laughed. "Even with red hair, Amanda wouldn't look anything like me, ID or not."

"Roberto would have killed you and Katharine, Nana," Lauren said. "He's a sociopath." There were a few of them running around Palmetto Beach, Kate thought. "He killed Grace because that private detective she'd hired had found out about Roberto's smuggling operation, and he slit his rich mistress's throat because she'd served her purpose."

"I think Grace may have been murdered because she'd discovered her daughter wasn't dead," Kate said. "She probably saw through Amanda's Diamond Lil disguise, recognized her daughter's eyes. They were so like Grace's."

"Detective Carbone, I'm so sorry I didn't tell you I'd gone to Grace Rowling's room on Monday night," Jennifer said. "I thought Jon Michael might harm Katharine and that Grace knew more than she'd told me. I made a bad judgment call, the deal in Bangkok was coming to a head, and I didn't want to be stuck in Palmetto Beach as a prime suspect."

Kevin, who was sitting between his wife and his younger daughter, put an arm around each of them.

Katharine reached over and patted her mother's hand. Nick just grunted.

"Talking about sociopaths," Marlene said, changing the subject, "Amanda aided and abetted her own mother's murder."

"But Jon Michael was murdered because Roberto had overheard me talking about my inheritance." Katharine sounded ashamed.

"Well, that was one reason. It's complicated," Nick said.

"Jon Michael believed Amanda had been murdered and he was the prime suspect. He also believed Roberto was his friend who'd protected him and given him an alibi. He felt he owed Roberto big-time. Then he found out Amanda was alive and Roberto had been using him. Jon Michael became a threat, and Roberto wasn't about to divide the money three ways. Hell, Roberto had Claude begging to become a smuggler. Roberto rigged the wire cage's opening so the pig's blood would seep out of the plastic bag and into the ocean."

"Now it's over," Jennifer said, and turned to her daughter. "Are you coming home?"

Kate heard the nervousness in her daughter-in-law's voice.

"Yes," Katharine said. "I'm going back to NYU. Nana, I'm going to write a screenplay about all this. Want to hear the title?"

"Yes, darling." Kate laughed. It felt good.

"*Death Rides the Surf*. And I'll get Mary Tyler Moore and Valerie Harper to play you and Marlene." Katharine looked at Nick. "And Paul Sorvino can play you."

"As long as I get the girl," Nick said.

Decades ago, Marlene had accepted her guilt over the one-night stand with Charlie. She'd even written Kate a letter confessing the adultery to be opened after Marlene's death.

Now that they were so much older, Marlene felt she should suffer the guilt alone. Why should she hurt her best friend?

She mixed a martini, opened a pack of Virginia Slims, lit a match and burned the letter.

Photo by Matthew Holler

Noreen Wald

Noreen Wald lives in downtown Sarasota, Florida with her husband, Steve. Their sons visit often. Hey, surf and sun are great lures. She has served terms as a local chapter president for Mystery Writers of America, as well as Executive VP and Secretary for their National Board of Directors. A winning contestant on seven television game shows—including Jeopardy!—Noreen later worked for Goodson-Todman and Merv Griffin Productions. She's lectured at the Smithsonian, the CIA , the National Press Club and aboard the QE II. Her Ghostwriter Series was a Mystery Guild selection and praised in *The New York Daily News, The Sun-Sentinel*, and hit #1 on *The Dallas Morning News* bestseller list.

The Kate Kennedy Mystery Series
By Noreen Wald

DEATH WITH AN OCEAN VIEW (#1)
DEATH OF THE SWAMI SCHWARTZ (#2)
DEATH IS A BARGAIN (#3)
DEATH STORMS THE SHORE (#4)
DEATH RIDES THE SURF (#5)

Available at booksellers nationwide and online

Visit www.henerypress.com for details

Henery Press Mystery Books

And finally, before you go…
Here are a few other mysteries
you might enjoy:

GHOSTWRITER ANONYMOUS
Noreen Wald

A Jake O'Hara Mystery (#1)

With her books sporting other people's names, ghostwriter Jake O'Hara works behind the scenes. But she never expected a séance at a New York apartment to be part of her job. Jake had signed on as a ghostwriter, secretly writing for a grande dame of mystery fiction whose talent died before she did. The author's East Side residence was impressive. But her entourage—from a Mrs. Danvers-like housekeeper to a lurking hypnotherapist—was creepy.

Still, it was all in a day's work, until a killer started going after ghostwriters, and Jake suspected she was chillingly close to the culprit. Attending a séance and asking the dead for spiritual help was one option. Some brilliant sleuthing was another-before Jake's next deadline turns out to be her own funeral.

Available at booksellers nationwide and online

Visit www.henerypress.com for details

MACDEATH
Cindy Brown

An Ivy Meadows Mystery (#1)

Like every actor, Ivy Meadows knows that *Macbeth* is cursed. But she's finally scored her big break, cast as an acrobatic witch in a circus-themed production of *Macbeth* in Phoenix, Arizona. And though it may not be Broadway, nothing can dampen her enthusiasm—not her flying cauldron, too-tight leotard, or carrot-wielding dictator of a director.

But when one of the cast dies on opening night, Ivy is sure the seeming accident is "murder most foul" and that she's the perfect person to solve the crime (after all, she does work part-time in her uncle's detective agency). Undeterred by a poisoned Big Gulp, the threat of being blackballed, and the suddenly too-real curse, Ivy pursues the truth at the risk of her hard-won career—and her life.

Available at booksellers nationwide and online

Visit www.henerypress.com for details

DEATH BY BLUE WATER
Kait Carson

A Hayden Kent Mystery (#1)

Paralegal Hayden Kent knows first-hand that life in the Florida Keys can change from perfect to perilous in a heartbeat. When she discovers a man's body at 120' beneath the sea, she thinks she is witness to a tragic accident. She becomes the prime suspect when the victim is revealed to be the brother of the man who recently jilted her, and she has no alibi. A migraine stole Hayden's memory of the night of the death.

As the evidence mounts, she joins forces with an Officer Janice Kirby. Together the two women follow the clues that uncover criminal activities at the highest levels and put Hayden's life in jeopardy while she fights to stay free.

Available at booksellers nationwide and online

Visit www.henerypress.com for details

MURDER ON A SILVER PLATTER
Shawn Reilly Simmons

A Red Carpet Catering Mystery (#1)

Penelope Sutherland and her Red Carpet Catering company just got their big break as the on-set caterer for an upcoming blockbuster. But when she discovers a dead body outside her house, Penelope finds herself in hot water. Things start to boil over when serious accidents threaten the lives of the cast and crew. And when the film's star, who happens to be Penelope's best friend, is poisoned, the entire production is nearly shut down.

Threats and accusations send Penelope out of the frying pan and into the fire as she struggles to keep her company afloat. Before Penelope can dish up dessert, she must find the killer or she'll be the one served up on a silver platter.

Available at booksellers nationwide and online

Visit www.henerypress.com for details

LOWCOUNTRY BOIL
Susan M. Boyer

A Liz Talbot Mystery (#1)

Private Investigator Liz Talbot is a modern Southern belle: she blesses hearts and takes names. She carries her Sig 9 in her Kate Spade handbag, and her golden retriever, Rhett, rides shotgun in her hybrid Escape. When her grandmother is murdered, Liz hightails it back to her South Carolina island home to find the killer.

She's fit to be tied when her police-chief brother shuts her out of the investigation, so she opens her own. Then her long-dead best friend pops in and things really get complicated. When more folks start turning up dead in this small seaside town, Liz must use more than just her wits and charm to keep her family safe, chase down clues from the hereafter, and catch a psychopath before he catches her.

Available at booksellers nationwide and online

Visit www.henerypress.com for details

Printed in the USA
CPSIA information can be obtained
at www.ICGtesting.com
LVHW011333051223
703742LV00023B/113/J